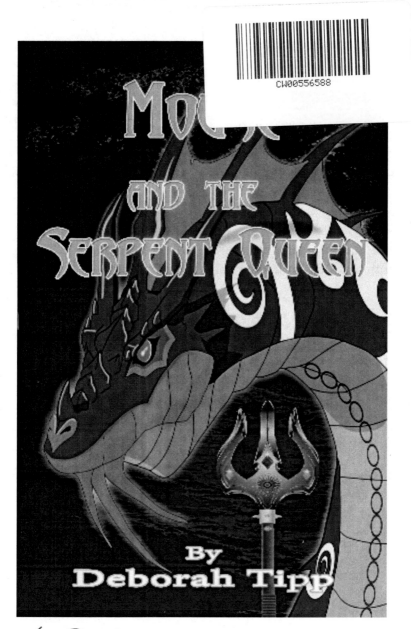

MOGUR
AND THE
SERPENT QUEEN

By
Deborah Tipp

To Bella
Happy 8th Birthday!
Love from Debbie xx

Published in February 2014 by emp3books,
Norwood House, Elvetham Road, Fleet, GU51 4HL,
England

©Deborah Tipp

ISBN-13: 978-1-907140-87-7

This book is also available on Kindle through Amazon

Other books by this author include:
Mouse and the Dragon Crystal

Acknowledgements

I would like to thank Rich, Maffs, Jords and Samuel for supporting me through a second episode of sitting on my own quietly, hogging the PC and constantly going on about my books! They're all glad I have my own laptop now !

Andy from Tikimax Digital Design has continued to be a massive help, and is now in fact a good friend. I thank him for the hard work he put into getting the second book cover just right and influencing my imagination when it came to the way I saw the serpents.

My Mum, Sister, Dad, Grammy and Brother have also continued to provide me with a never ending supply of love and enthusiasm and encouraged me to keep living my dream.

I'd also like to thank my 'proof reader' Ben ... thankyou so much for your time and support.

All of you have made my dreams come true....

Please visit my website for further info.

www.deborahtipp.co.uk

I would like to dedicate this book to my wonderful husband and step-son

Rich and Samuel Tipp

And to two amazingly brave women - Linda and Marie

.... Never Forgotten

<u>Chapter One</u>

As Mouse stood at the edge of the park looking at the big old tree, the six months since she had last been here, seemed dull in comparison.

She had enjoyed starting her new school, making new friends and getting used to village life but her adventure with her Dragon friends had made normal life seem just that little bit mundane.

*

Mouse had gone back home to her mum and dad, on that bright September day, a little dazed but she was also jubilant to see that the village had remained exactly the same as she'd left it. When she got to her house, she had found her mum and dad, hugged them tight and enjoyed the rest of her birthday glued to their sides!

A few days later she had gone back to the art studio and

with some of her birthday money, bought her favourite small picture of the willow tree and placed it in her bedroom on her dressing table. She had found a little red gift bag, wrapped her red crystal in tissue and put it inside the gift bag. She had then taped it to the back of the frame so no one could see it. Only her, when she needed to.

Every so often, over the last six months, she had stolen moments to remember her dragon friends whilst holding the red crystal in her hands. It almost felt like she could feel them all, in the palm of her hand, just by holding the small shiny stone.

*

Her first day at school had been nerve-wracking, being the new girl to the village, but she had been welcomed warmly. As far as school was concerned, she had got used to the timetable of different lessons and was in the top percentage of her class for most subjects. She had been studious and focused and enjoyed all the lessons but her favourite, quite obviously, was art.

She had made some good friends who had helped her cope well with the new lessons that senior school demanded. She had slotted into a pre-formed group of girls who all liked to read and to paint. There were three of them; Amelia, Jade and Megan and they all lived in Willowdown. Once Mouse had spent some time getting to know them during school, they had started to meet up outside school going to the small village cinema, having sleep-overs and of course, finding spots to paint and draw.

One, not so cold day in early October, Mouse's dad had driven the four girls to the beach where they had spent the time drawing and painting and eating delicious ice-creams. Mouse's dad had finished off the day by taking them all to a seaside fish and chip restaurant and treated them all to tea before driving back to the village.

The girls had all painted one picture each that day, they chatted on the fairly long journey home, about each doing four good pictures over the next few months, and having an art stall at the Christmas Fayre.

Mouse enjoyed the company of all three girls but had formed a special bond with Megan and had nearly told her, on numerous occasions, about her secret adventure. She had stopped herself just in time. Her new friend would either not believe her, or worse, think she was insane!

One day, maybe, she would tell her.

Winter had come and gone and Christmas in the village had been bright and festive. The girls had all managed to produce four pictures each and had their own stall at the Christmas Fayre. By the end of the day there were no pictures left to sell and the girls were excited to have earnt some money, albeit a small amount each, from all their hard work. The local drama group had produced a pantomime – Aladdin – and the whole school had gone to watch it. Mouse loved the community spirit of this village, where everyone supported everyone, something she had not been used to when she had lived in the city.

*

So here, now, as she gazed at the tree, she wondered what would happen when she drew another picture whilst encased in the trees cocoon like branches.

Was it a one off?

3

Would it happen again?

More importantly, what would she draw this time, knowing the possible consequences?

She admitted to herself that she was a little nervous, "Come on Molly, move!" She muttered to herself, as she stood a few feet away from the great tree. She realised that the tree wasn't the only thing around that was rooted to the spot!

Dragons.

Swords.

Death.

All the memories of Mullar, Veccy, Jaymor and Taya; of the village, their little stonelet, the delicious food and how welcome they had made her feel in the unusual world she had found herself in. She remembered being whisked off high into the sky, once on the back of a sturdy hunter and then on the back of Zable.

Zable.

He had died to save her, and to save her new friends' world.

The memories became a blur of swirling images as she stood still, memories that stopped her from taking another step.

Snapping herself out of her daydream, she ventured forward, one slow step at a time until her hands could reach out and touch the weeping branches.

Without being conscious of her actions, lost in the magic of the tree, she then found herself inside the tree's dome. And like before, it was cooler out of the mid-morning sunshine.

She looked around her, the branches weren't quite as 'full' as before but then it was still only early Spring and this was only the third or fourth really warm day they'd had this year. Within a month or so the long dangly branches would fill out and only sprinkle shafts of sunlight when a light breeze allowed.

Today though, plenty of warm light was penetrating through the slightly sparse, rope like branches.

As Mouse sat herself down, in the same place as before, she allowed herself a deep breath.

"Ok," she sighed, "here we go."

She began to arrange her pad, her water and her artists' box around her. She had mastered the art of watercolours over the last few months and decided to try something different today.

Pastels.

Mouse knew what she wanted to draw but knowing the magic this old tree possessed, she was a little nervous.

She wanted to draw a mermaid.

She had the vision in her head of how she wanted her picture to look; the colours, the shapes, the lines. However, she knew that drawing such a picture, of something that lived under water, could be very dangerous for her if she was to be transported to an underwater world!

Mouse almost laughed out loud – she decided that if she could escape from fire breathing dragons and actually have the courage to stab one with a spear, then a mermaid would be a piece of cake to deal with.

Mouse got out the necessary items from her box and arranged them in the order she would need them. She settled down with a blank page in front of her. Before starting her picture, Mouse closed her eyes and let her hands move across the paper, feeling it, and helping her formulate an image. She let colours and shapes invade her mind, her imagination being carried on a wave of ideas.

Eyes open, she was ready.

She began by rubbing some blue and green pastels on their sides across the whole page making a watery coloured background, and then, with her rubber she erased a space for her mermaid.

She drew the outline with a light pencil, just to get the right perspective, she would add the detailing of seaweed and colourful fish at the end. Once she was happy with the basic outline, she chose her pastel colours and began to fill in the tail. She chose pale blues, greens and specs of white to make it look like it was shimmering in the water.

With her finger she began to rub all the colours in together making a turquoise which, when the specs of white were added, brought the long elegant tail to life. She moved up to the body and although she had a flesh coloured pastel, she added some pale green to give a watery reflection on the skin.

She had drawn the stereotypical scallop shells on the chest area and coloured them in pinks and creams. She left the face fairly undefined but drew masses of golden hair fanning the face and made it look like it was swooshing around in the water.

She stopped for a moment and held the picture at arm's length, reviewing her progress. Satisfied that it was coming along nicely, she carried on smudging colours together and adding specs of white here and there until there was no more needed to be done to the actual mermaid itself.

She spent the next half an hour drawing wavy seaweed in different colours and some fish in shoals around the mermaid.

Finally happy that her picture was finished, she gazed down upon the beautiful mermaid. It was a lovely picture, with depth and definition, she was very pleased with it.

And so, with some trepidation, she waited.

And waited.

Mouse checked the time on her phone, it was 10.45am and as she put her phone back in her pocket, a familiar feeling crept over her.

With wide eyes she watched the long, once lifeless, branches begin to sparkle; twinkling lights blinding her for a moment. She saw them start to sway, slowly at first, then faster and faster, as they spun around her.

Mouse wasn't sure if it was the blinding, sparkling lights or the rapid spinning of the branches but she felt that recognisable feeling of dizziness.

*

As Mouse opened her eyes the twinkling and swaying branches began to subside and she was able to focus properly once again.

As the branches came to a standstill and the swishing noise stopped, Mouse realised how very hot it was all of a sudden. The light outside the flimsy branches was incredibly bright, leaving no protection from the instant heat she now felt.

Tentatively she looked down on the grass beside her, to where her pad lay.

Once again her original picture had transformed itself but this time, as she stared at the new image, she was suddenly quite afraid.

Her beautiful colourful mermaid with long golden hair had turned into an evil looking half human, half eel like creature! Just looking at it gave Mouse the shivers.

The face was grey, crowned with long black hair, the body was like her mermaid but it was a pale and lifeless green/grey colour. The most horrifying thing about the transformation was the tail; it was sleek, black and slippery looking with spiny fins running down the full length of it! All in all, the creature was dark and menacing.

Mouse didn't know what to do next. She knew that drawing a picture of home wouldn't work, and she knew that somehow she would need to find someone – or something – to get her back.

What had she done?

In her panic, she started to busy herself with packing up her pastels and her pad. She didn't need to keep looking at the new picture – it was etched in her mind. She put everything away neatly in her box, along with her phone, and once again hid the box under some fallen leaves beside the tree.

She stood up, on slightly shaky legs, and cautiously took steps towards the branches, the thought of the hideous eel creature at the fore front of her mind. She reached out her hand and pulled back the thin curtain of leaves to reveal the new world which she was now a part of.

The colours, smells and a terrific thump of heat hit her instantly.

"A jungle?" She exclaimed, not really understanding the connection of a mermaid and a jungle!

As she looked about her, she saw greens, reds, oranges and yellows in all the different strange looking plants and flowers. There were small shrubs, large trees and flowers with leaves that were nearly as big as her! She gazed upwards, following a tree trunk which rose from the soft mossy ground, up and up, way into the sky where she had to shield her eyes from the brilliant sunshine. Eel creature forgotten for a moment, she stepped further away from 'her' tree. She looked back at it and realised how out of place it looked, with its sparse branches, compared to the lush vegetation surrounding it. It looked almost dead.

She slowly edged further away from 'her' tree, careful not to touch any foliage, and she could make out a clearing in the trees a little way ahead. She made her way towards it, curiosity overcoming fear.

As she reached the edge of the thick undergrowth she halted in her tracks.

What she saw before her took her breath away.

For there, stretching for what seemed like miles, was the most beautiful white sand shoreline she had ever seen! It looked just like the tropical beaches she had seen in her mum's magazines.

The sea was gently rippling along the sand, leaving silvery white foamy trails along the edge of the water. When the sunlight caught the trails of foam, it looked like someone had dropped small diamonds along the length of the shore, glistening in the light.

She noticed that the thick undergrowth hugged the shoreline as far as the eye could see, except for a small break in the trees which allowed a small river to join the ocean.

Mouse looked all about her before venturing out of the security of the jungle. Confident that she was alone for now, she stepped onto the sand, bent down and scooped up a handful of powdery grains. She let it slip through her fingers, it was warm and soft.

She plopped herself down and took in the sight before her. The sun was high in the clear blue sky, the sea was a calm, aqua, shimmering surface and the sand looked undisturbed in its tranquil beauty.

It was at that moment, with everything being so still and untouched, that she realised that she hadn't seen any sign of life here yet. There were no footprints in the sand, no splashing in the water and absolutely no evidence of anyone having been here before her.

Was she all alone on this island?

Was she scared?

And what on earth did her picture mean?

She leant forward and stared at the sea, half hoping to see a flick of a tail or a ripple on the surface of the water. But there was nothing.

Mouse sighed and took off her shoes, buried her toes in the sand and wiggled them about. It tickled but the sand was warm and it felt good. She lay back, bathing in the warmth of the sun, and closed her eyes. It was so peaceful and so relaxing that she'd forgotten all about the picture transformation of only half an hour ago.

She allowed herself to think of her dragon friends, who she missed terribly sometimes when she was alone. And at this precise moment she felt very alone.

She thought about Taya and Jaymor and what they would make of the sea and the sunshine. They would have swooped off and within minutes would have been small dark silhouettes against the blue of the sky. They would be twirling and soaring and enjoying the freedom that flying allowed.

This world being such a different colour from theirs; this, vibrant and alive, theirs, dusky and dull. How she wished they could be here.

It didn't occur to Mouse that she hadn't wished her new

school friends were there.

Suddenly Mouse's eyes were wide open!

Somewhere behind her she'd heard a snap of a twig, or something.

Alert now, she sat bolt upright and slipped her shoes on.

There it was again.

The feeling of being alone certainly had its benefits.

After her eyes had been closed for some time, she struggled to focus in the bright sunlight and couldn't see anything at first, in the dense vegetation. Everything seems statuesque. There wasn't even a breeze to move the smallest of leaf.

Mouse held her breath for what seemed like ages, but still saw nothing. All was quiet once again.

Mouse stood up slowly and moved quietly towards the trees trying to see and figure out what had moved and made the noise.

Then with a flash of speed, something leapt out from behind a tree and disappeared deeper into the jungle!

Without thinking Mouse chased after it.

It was moving quickly and Mouse found it hard to keep up. She still had no clear view of exactly what it was she was chasing.

'It' sped amongst the dense terrain and Mouse followed the bushes and plants which moved in its wake. Branches and leaves were brushing against her face, arms and legs. Boulders loomed from nowhere to slow her down, but she battled on, forgetting to be careful about not touching anything. It wasn't easy to keep up as this was unfamiliar territory to her but she kept the moving target in her sights – just.

The only clear image she glimpsed was lots of thick white

hair billowing behind whatever speedy body it belonged to.

Thankfully the vegetation was beginning to thin out but what Mouse didn't see was a twisted branch looping up from the ground and it snagged her foot and sent her sprawling to the floor with a yelp. She had cut her ankle and blood was trickling down her heel.

Determined and desperate to carry on and not lose this race, she freed her foot and kept going. She wasn't able to go as fast, practically reduced to a hobble but she finally got to the edge of the trees just in time to see a long, thin pair of legs disappear, with a small splash, into a large pool of deep, dark water.

***

<u>Chapter Two</u>

As Mouse limped towards the edge of the pool, the ripples from the splash had stopped and she was left staring at a picturesque lagoon with a waterfall at one end and completely surrounded with the now familiar lush green and colourful vegetation.

"Wow" she whispered to herself, thinking that this would be beautiful to paint. The colours were so vibrant and she could probably paint about three or four pictures, all of different areas, just from this one lagoon!

Suddenly remembering what had just happened, she frantically searched the water for any sign of the legs that had dived into this serene pool only moments ago.

Only when she took a step further towards the pool, balancing on a boulder, did she cry out in pain; a painful reminder of the stumble over the branch.

Without moving she scanned immediate area. The lagoon was a deep blue and mainly still. The waterfall giving off the only noise, and causing ripples as the water rushed down a jagged rock face and into the pool. There were a few small rocky areas around the edge of the pool, providing shallower water, like small shingle beaches, but it was mainly green leafy tendrils which formed a lace like pattern, delicately draped around the water's edge.

With wide eyes, Mouse cautiously moved towards one of the shallower areas of the lagoon where she could bathe her ankle. Apart from the constant gushing of the waterfall, she could hear nothing.

She sat down carefully, on a large boulder which was half in the water and half out. She took off her shoe and flexed her ankle to the left and right. It hurt a little but it wasn't too bad.

As she slowly dipped her foot into the water she realised how hot she was and so she took off the other shoe and dipped her other foot in too. The water was cool and refreshing and she instantly felt calmed.

Mouse leant forward and cupped some water in her hand and let it trickle over the cut on her ankle. She winced as it touched the raw graze but it soon felt much better and she relished the coolness on her feet as she swished them to and fro.

What Mouse hadn't noticed while being transfixed with the water, was a little blonde head bobbing on the surface of the water, just in front of the waterfall.

*

Mouse was happily humming to herself; the mysterious

creature she had chased through the jungle was at the back of her mind as she succumbed to the hypnotising serenity of the lagoon.

She swooshed her feet in the water and splashed it on her hands and face to cool down and refresh herself.

Mouse stopped humming as she thought she heard a rustling noise behind her, she thought about the earlier chase and decided there was no way she was going to manage *that* again so she remained sat down. It went quiet again and she decided she must have imagined it.

She snapped her head round at a 'closer' noise just in time to see a huge scaly beast start his charge towards her!

Mouse leapt to her feet and screamed.

The beast bared his sharp teeth, drool slapping at the side of his enormous jaws, his huge body thumping at the ground as he sped towards her.

Mouse was unable to move through sheer panic.

Before Mouse had time to react, she was grabbed by the legs from behind and hauled into the water, just as the beast's mouth clamped shut with a crash – missing her by inches!

With a cough and a splutter, Mouse resurfaced and took a deep breath. She pushed her hair from her face and stared straight into the snarling face of the beast. He stood on the very rock she had been sat on, his huge scaly feet armed with pointed talons, his drooling mouth gnashing and his dark eyes staring.

"Oh ... oh" stammered Mouse, her eyes wide with terror.

In her sheer panic she hadn't realised that she was still being 'hugged' by someone/something.

The grip around her loosened from behind and the movement of the water suggested that whoever had rescued her was now a few feet away. Mouse kept very still, the beast was still only a few feet away and she could smell his breath every time he snorted, a foul stench she wished she couldn't smell. The beast just stared at her with his mouth open.

Without warning the beast snapped his mouth shut so hard and fast that the crunching sound echoed around the lagoon!

Mouse let out a shocked scream and threw herself further backwards into the water, with a splash, and once again into the arms of the unknown.

She let the long arms wrap themselves around her quivering body, grateful of the support, but she could not take her eyes off the beast.

Mouse and the beast.....Staring at each other in silence, a battle of wills, one hungry, the other petrified.

But the beast knew when he was beaten and Mouse knew that he obviously couldn't swim!

The beast looked at his 'dinner' for the last time, stomped his huge feet on the rock, huffed and backed away into the jungle.

Mouse hadn't been aware that she had been holding her breath until a great sigh escaped her and her ribcage felt its normal size once again.

To say that Mouse was scared was an understatement but she knew she had to turn around and face whatever was still clutching her.

She straightened out her legs and, much to her relief; she discovered that she could just about touch the bottom.

So on tippy toes she slowly turned round to face her rescuer.

She saw a girl, not a mermaid, but a girl who still had hold of her.

It was the long white hair she noticed and recognised first, and then she saw the enormous round blue eyes set in a pale heart shaped face.

They just stared at each other for a moment and then Mouse smiled. The girl smiled back; a big wide smile which revealed lots of small pointy teeth, top and bottom.

"Um ... thank you." Said Mouse.

The big eyes blinked.

"You were nearly his snack!" Replied the girl.

"What *was* it?!

"One of the Verzillas."

"What's one of those, and there are more of them?"

"There are about 20 of them in the herd, and they are one of the longest surviving creatures on this island. He must have been an older one because the young males would never have been too slow to miss a kill."

Mouse shuddered.

"Oh." Was all she could manage.

The girl noticed Mouse shudder. "Are you cold?" She asked.

"Um ... no. I'm just a bit shocked, that's all."

The girl let go of Mouse but Mouse panicked and clung back onto her.

"It's ok," said the girl, "he won't come in here, he can't swim."

"Sorry," replied Mouse, "it's just that I haven't seen one of those before!"

The girl smiled an even wider smile and said, "And I've never seen one of you before."

Mouse didn't quite understand what the girl meant but before she could ask her, the girl had started to swim them

17

over to the other side of the lagoon. The girl saw the look of horror in Mouse's eyes as the neared the shore, "It's ok, they cannot get over this side of the island, you're quite safe."

Mouse visibly relaxed and let the girl help her out of the water and onto a small pebbly area where she unceremoniously plopped herself down in heavy wet clothes.

She watched the girl get out of the water and then understood what she had meant earlier about having not seen a human before.

Mouse noticed how long the girl's arms were, how incredibly long her legs were and how both her fingers and toes were webbed, her feet looked almost like flippers! The girl was wearing what looked like a skirted swimming costume made out of a shiny rubbery material in a deep green colour. The mass of long white hair was a stark contrast to the dark green of her outfit which was a little scary until you looked into the girl's huge eyes, which were of the softest blue. The pale, almost translucent skin of her face enhancing the delicate blue of her eyes and the soft whiteness of her hair.

But as the girl bent down to sit beside Mouse, an opening on the back of the outfit, running down the centre of her spine, revealed an elegant flimsy dorsal fin! It was almost un-noticeable in the sunlight because it was so thin but the colours – turquoises, purples and reds – glistened as she moved.

The two girls sat together in silence for a few minutes, gathering their thoughts and warming their bodies through in the sunshine.

"By the way, I'm Mouse." Announced Mouse, a little

uncomfortable with the silence.

"I'm Angel."

"That's a very pretty name."

"Thank you, it was my mum's name too."

"Well, my real name is Molly but everyone calls me Mouse," as she looked at Angel and saw confusion, she followed by saying "it's a long story, never mind."

The girls fell silent once again.

"How did you find us?" Asked Angel.

Mouse looked at Angel, "Well that's a bit of a story too," she smiled, "and it involves a magic tree."

That got Angel's attention as she sat bolt upright, towering over Mouse, "Where? Here on Volmère?"

"Volmère?" Questioned Mouse.

"Yes, this island is called Volmère. It's name comes from the Volcanic Island of the Sea Mermaids."

"Mermaids." Mouse muttered.

"Yes mermaids. Now tell me about this tree. Where is it, why is it magic and can you take me to see it?" Angel was up on her feet, her long webbed feet, pacing around the small pebbly area by the water.

"Well I would show you it but I am not going back over there where that hungry beast thing is!"

Angel looked disappointed at first but then agreed that to venture back over to that side of the lagoon so soon would be far too dangerous, "You can show me another day perhaps." She sat back down close to Mouse.

"Mmmm, maybe."

"I never realised we had a magic tree here on the island!" Angel squealed.

"Well I came across it by accident a few months ago when I wanted to find a quiet spot to paint my pictures. I sat down under the big old willow tree in my village and ended up being whisked away to another world!"

Angel's face was agog, "You mean this has happened before?"

"Yes it has."

"Where did you end up that time?"

"Oh it was a world where half dragon, half humans lived and there was an ancient old dragon who was hundreds of years old."

"Wow ... Dragons!" Gasped Angel, "But how did you make the tree magic?"

Mouse smiled at Angel, "I have no idea, I just drew a picture of a real dragon the last time and within minutes my picture had changed into a half dragon, half human and I was in another world!"

"So what did you draw this time – to get here?"

"A mermaid."

"Oh," said Angel, "and what did that change into?"

Mouse's face clouded over a little.

"It turned into a dark, evil looking eel like creature, all spiny and horrid."

This time it was Angel's face that darkened.

"I think your picture turned into the Serpent Queen, Inanya."

"Who is she, and what has she got to do with my beautiful mermaid?"

"That is a long story and I'll let my dad tell you all about it, but right now I have to get back in the water, this sun is no good for my skin."

And with that she dove head first into the pool again, leaving Mouse standing on the small beachy area wondering what to do next.

Mouse watched Angel as she swam deftly under the water towards the waterfall. She surfaced just in front of the crashing waterfall and waved for Mouse to follow her.

Mouse looked down at her nearly dry clothes and decided to see if she could get to the waterfall on foot, along the water's edge, and stay dry. But without her shoes it could be hard going and a little uncomfortable.

As she stood up, her ankle felt a little stiff but the warmth had dried up the graze and her foot was much easier to stand on. She started to navigate the terrain barefoot but it soon became clear that there was no way she would make it all the way round the side of the pool without getting back into the water.

"Mouse! Mouse! Come on!" Encouraged Angel, "Get in the water – it's the only way."

Mouse stopped in her tracks to survey her progress so far, and reluctantly agreed with Angel. The little pebbly area where they had sat had petered out after a few feet and became a rugged path with loose shingle and sharp drops into the water.

"Ok," said Mouse, "I'm coming!" And as she looked again to where Angel was treading water, she spotted two other little white heads bobbing about near to the waterfall.

Angel noticed that Mouse was hesitating, and followed her gaze to the additional bobbing heads which had just appeared.

"It's ok Mouse. This is my brother and sister."

Mouse looked at the three pale heart shaped faces, all smiling toothy smiles at her and realised that she'd been in worse situations than this, so she grabbed hold of her nose and jumped into the cool water with a plop!

As she surfaced, she had been joined by Angel's brother

and sister, who didn't say a word but quite unashamedly just stared at her.

"Come, let's get you out of the water and home to meet everyone."

"Home?" Mouse spluttered as Angel made her way towards the waterfall.

"Yes, my village, Bichir, is just the other side of the fall. It's warm inside and you can dry off properly."

Mouse hadn't quite worked out how by going into a waterfall, then presumably a cave, it could be anywhere near dry and warm but she didn't really have any other options.

Somewhat amazed but not really scared, Mouse followed the three siblings towards the splashing foam. All three effortlessly ducked their heads down and went under the spray leaving Mouse treading water on her own.

She searched the width of the waterfall but couldn't see a spot which was less forceful. She swam to the left and felt around the rock for a let up in the torrent but this side seemed even more energetic than the front so she swam back to the middle and waited.

Angel's white head surfaced, "What are you waiting for, come on!"

"I'm not sure about swimming through a waterfall, I've never done it before."

Realisation dawned on Angel, "Goodness, sorry Mouse. Here, go to the right and there is a tiny gap in the rock face where you can dodge the water and squeeze through to Bichir."

Gratefully Mouse swam round to the right and sure enough there was an area of rock which looked to be chiselled out, enough for her to pass through without having the thunderous water batter at her.

As she clung onto the rock and pulled herself through the gap, only her face got wet from the spray, she found herself in an inner lagoon. And although this wasn't as green as the one she had just left, it was even more breathtaking because of the richness of the colours whose defiance against the lack of full sun light, truly astonished her.

She watched as Angel and her brother and sister swam into the centre of the pool which was spot-lighted by shafts of light from up above. And although she couldn't actually see the sun from where she was, there were great beams of light pouring in for her to be able to take in the unusual surroundings she found herself in.

She remained just inside the waterfall, treading water, taking in what could only be described as a cave village, surrounding a beautiful clear pool.

As her eyes swept around the scenery before her she spotted oval shaped holes dug out of the craggy rock, at various heights all around. She saw curtains of vegetation draped along the rock which did not look dissimilar to the sparse branches of her willow tree. At the opposite end of the waterfall was a large beach like area which was also bathed in a large shaft of light streaming in from a large hole in the ceiling of the cave. The sand was the same as the powdery, soft, white sand of the beach she had been on earlier; each grain seeming to shimmer and glisten, lighting up the edge of the pool.

As an art lover, Mouse appreciated the natural surroundings, the captivating beauty of the unlikely spot and felt the strong, familiar desire to capture the vision on paper.

Only when her mind had processed the surroundings, did she notice that the cave was bustling with activity. Angel and her brother and sister had swum across the pool to the beach area and were wading through the shallow water onto the sand.

Angel turned to face the waterfall finally, and waved to Mouse, who was still treading water at the other end.

The pool was about 75 metres from the waterfall to the beach, and Mouse suddenly felt cold, so she started to swim towards Angel.

Angel had now been joined by most of the villagers, and was standing next to an older man who had his arms draped over her shoulder and her brother and sister.

As Mouse swam all she could see in front of her was a gathering of white hair! Every single villager, without exception, had the same hair as Angel but worn at different lengths.

Angel sploshed back into the water to meet Mouse as she got closer to the beach. Mouse was a little bit overwhelmed with everyone staring at her. But Angel took her hand and they walked up the beach together.

"This is Mouse everyone, and she came to our island by drawing a picture of a mermaid under a magic tree!" Announced Angel.

There were a number of 'oooohs' and 'ahhhhs' amongst the crowd and the older man stepped forward and offered his hand to Mouse, "I'm Arowan, Angel's dad. Pleased to meet you Mouse." He said.

"Um, hello." Replied Mouse as she shook his hand.

"I'd like to hear more about this magic tree if that's ok?"

"Um, sure." Replied Mouse. She looked around at all the faces who were gazing at her, almost transfixed, and

24

Mouse managed a weak smile. The females were all wearing a similar costume to Angel – all the same style but in different shades, and the men just wore the bottom half of the garment – they reminded her of the pictures she'd seen as a child, of Tarzan. And as amusing as she found it, she was still a bit shaken up by her recent encounter with the Verzilla, so she was able to control the urge to giggle.

Arowan picked up on her discomfort and turned to the villagers and said, "Right everyone, off you go, we'll have our usual gathering on the beach here tonight and welcome Mouse properly." And with a waving of his hands he shooed the crowd away.

Obediently all the pale, heart shaped faces nodded and moved away.

"Angel, get something for Mouse to wear so she can get out of her wet clothes, she looks half frozen to death." Instructed Arowan.

"Yes dad," Angel nodded, "come with me Mouse and let's see if I can find you something to change into."

As Arowan turned to leave them, Mouse noticed that the fin on his back was obviously larger than Angel's but the shades were slightly darker with the very tips streaked in black.

Angel and Mouse left Arowan issuing further instructions to a few of the men to go out fishing once again to try to catch something a little special for tonight's feast. He had put his arm round his other two children and moved towards an inner cave within the lagoon village.

"Will you have something to fit me Angel?" Mouse asked, "You're an awful lot taller than me."

"I think I have a few smaller suits which I wore a few months ago which should still be ok to wear and may possibly fit you."

"Ok." Said Mouse as she followed Angel towards the same cave as her dad had disappeared into, but at the last minute, veered off to a separate cave next door.

"This is my very own dwelling." Announced Angel proudly, "My dad thought I was old enough to have my own place now, as long as it was next to his." She smiled.

Mouse shivered as she stepped into the coolness of the smaller cave and couldn't wait to get on some fresh clothes and get back out into the sunshine.

As her eyes adjusted to the dimmer light, Mouse discovered a truly girls theme to what could have just been a hole in the rock face. Angel's dwelling was about the same size as her own bedroom back at home, and had a large raised area in the rock, at the back of the cave, for a bed. It was covered over by, what could only be described as, a woven leaf blanket and the whole thing looked incredibly uncomfortable to Mouse. Around the dwelling, there were boulders of different sizes serving different purposes. All were flattened on the top but some had half coconut husks filled with shells and dried flowers, some had a selection of pouches and bowls whilst others looked as if they were for sitting on and had been arranged in a semi-circle.

And hung all around the walls were dried out flowers of all sizes and colours. There were also pretty coloured shells stuck to the walls, some on their own and others arranged in patterns.

"Wow Angel, it's lovely in here!" Exclaimed Mouse.

Pleased with Mouse's reaction, Angel grabbed her hand and led her to the back of the dwelling.

"Here," she said, as she made her way to a smaller hole

chiselled out of the cave, "I'll have a look for some smaller outfits for you." And with that she pulled out a neat pile of costumes all in the same green colour. Angel held up each costume in front of her and finally found the smallest one.

"This is the smallest one and it's still nice and flexible." She announced as she held it out for Mouse.

"Flexible?" Asked Mouse.

"Yes, after a while they dry out and perish but this one still looks ok to me."

"I've never heard of clothes that perish." Said Mouse.

"Well our outfits are made from a special plant grown here in the lagoon and last really well when we wear them in and out of the water all the time, but left to dry out too much and they just disintegrate."

"Oh I see," Said Mouse, who truthfully didn't 'see' at all, "so you have to keep popping in and out of the water just to keep your costumes wet?"

"Well sort of, but not just for that reason." Angel had put all the costumes back and had sat down on the hard looking bed, "we have to keep getting into the water to hydrate our skin too, and our fins. If we are out of the water for more than an hour or so we can get quite poorly and in extreme cases, die!"

"Oh!" Was all Mouse could say. She still didn't fully understand this tall beautiful girl who sat before her.

"So you have to get in the water all the time just so you don't die?"

Angel nodded.

"But what about going to sleep?"

"We don't sleep for long, the nights are short here, but we have a special layer on our beds, top and bottom, which keeps our skin hydrated." And she held up the woven blanket which looked wet and cold to Mouse.

"It doesn't look very warm and soft to me?"

"They are ok, we don't need much warmth here, it never seems to get very cold and we are used to them," Angel smiled, "what do you have on your bed at home then?"

"I have a soft, thick quilt which is like a thick dry blanket, which keeps me warm at night because where I come from it gets very cold sometimes."

"If these dry out we have to get a new one, they only last a few months. Once a week we leave them in the water to soak but they dry out eventually."

"So you get the plant from the water and then someone stitches them together?"

"Yes, they are woven to form the cover and then left in the water for a further day before we use them."

Mouse sat in silence for a moment or two digesting the information.

"Anyway," said Angel breaking the quietness in the dwelling and holding out the small costume, "I'll stitch the back up and you should be able to get into this easily."

Mouse watched her move around the cave, find a thick wooden needle and some twine and expertly stitch the hole in the back together.

"There," she said, "all done!" Angel held up the costume proudly.

"Shall I just get changed in here?" Asked Mouse.

"Yes, I'll just wait outside and drop the shades so no one can peek in." And with that Angel left Mouse alone to get out of her wet clothes and into a swimming costume made out of seaweed!

Mouse was now getting quite used to 'firsts'.

The costume fit perfectly and she emerged from the

dwelling feeling a lot less soggy, she also felt a lot cooler. The sun, although limited in the cave village, was still hot and she had felt wet and sticky in her own clothes. Unbelievably she felt refreshed in her seaweed outfit!

"Perfect!" Exclaimed Angel as she walked around Mouse.

"Thanks Angel. I've just draped my clothes over some boulders to dry off a bit."

"That's fine, we'll rinse them off properly tomorrow. But now, let's take a swim and I can show you around Bichir, our home."

The two girls smiled at each other, raced into the shallows and dove straight into the deep water.

Mouse was aware that she was still being observed by the many villagers although they were all desperately trying to conceal their interest.

"Right," said Angel as she pointed towards the oval holes in the cave walls that Mouse had noticed earlier, "all these dwellings are where everyone sleeps, mums, dads and children. The adults stay on the bottom layers with the smaller children and the older ones go above them."

"But how do the children get up there?" Asked Mouse as she pointed to one of the higher dwellings, "Some of them are really high up in the rock."

"We use the plants to climb up. We are all taught at an early age to climb, swim and fish."

Mouse laughed, "The children in that highest one must be really good at climbing then!"

Angel joined in, "Yes, they are. They are our village's strongest climbers and most successful fishers."

"Do you all go out into the sea then?"

"Every day nearly, but only once we've reached a certain age."

"Why's that?"

"It's very dangerous out there, especially for the younger ones who aren't strong swimmers so we have to be careful."

"And do you fish too Angel?"

"Yes, sometimes, I'm not the best, but I have a go."

They chatted on whilst they swam around the edge of the pool, attracting attention as they went. Angel explained who lived in the various dwellings and about what they all did with their days here on Volmère. Mouse found she was quite envious of her new friend's lifestyle; no school, no homework and no chores. Just swimming, fishing and collecting shells!

They had nearly completed the circuit, and the light was gradually fading, when there was an almighty screech followed by three separate splashes.

Shocked, Mouse immediately clung to Angel, who laughed at her and said, "Don't be scared, these are my friends."

And with that three white heads bobbed up to the surface and grinned at her.

"Mouse, meet Vimba, Bora and Tang."

Lessening her grip on Angel, Mouse half smiled back at the two girls and the boy who had just leapt into the pool.

"Where's Bonito?" Asked Angel.

"Oh, he's gone fishing with his dad, he'll be back soon." Replied the boy – Tang.

"Well Mouse and I are getting out now, before Mouse gets too cold, so we'll see you at the gathering in a bit."

They said their goodbyes and left them splashing about, whooping and diving in and out of the pool, curiosity of a human presence forgotten immediately.

As they walked back onto the warm sand a group of

villagers emerged from what looked like a tunnel in the side of the cave which Mouse hadn't spotted before, which fed directly into the pool, with a channel that lead onto the beach area. They were all carrying fish of various sizes presumably for the gathering and took them over to one side of the beach where some women had gathered together and were preparing skewers of vegetables and fruit. This was going to be some tea!

Over the next hour Mouse watched, sat on a rock by the pool, as everyone came together for the evening. A huge fire was started and a frame was constructed around it, and over it to cook the food on.

As the light from above wore out, a few of the adults produced large bowls in which they placed dry leaves and twigs. They gathered small branches from another plant and squeezed it over the leaves and twigs and used the main fire to light the bowls.

They placed the many bowls around the edge of the beach. It was a magical sight to behold and Mouse was thrilled to be part of it.

When Angel finally came and sat down next to Mouse after helping to prepare some of the fish and layer them over the frame, she asked, "What did they squeeze out of those branches into the bowls?"

"It's an oily extract that keeps the fires burning for longer." Replied Angel.

"Cool."

"Yeah, it is. Now, let's get sat down with the others, I'm starving!"

Mouse suddenly realised how hungry she was too. A sensation which was heightened in the next few minutes, as everyone gathered together to finish off cooking the

31

food, the delicious aromas making her mouth water.

The people of Bichir were warm and friendly and after a few moments of awkwardness they soon forgot that she was 'different' and welcomed her as if she was one of their own.

They all swapped stories about their days, shared their wonderful feast, relaxed and enjoyed the ambience of the evening. And it amused Mouse that every so often a group of them would disappear into the pool for a quick swim and then return to where they sat.

Halfway through this wonderful night, one of Angel's friends, Bonito who she hadn't met yet, asked her how she found them.

Silence dropped on Bichir like a heavy blanket and everyone looked at Mouse.

"Well," she started, "I just drew a picture of a mermaid, under a tree in my village and I was transported here, to you."

A million questions followed, not only about the picture and the tree but of Mouse and her home.

But silence returned and troubled expressions crossed the faces of the villagers when she mentioned the new picture on her pad earlier that day.

Mouse noticed and asked "What does that mean?" She looked around at everyone, "I mean, none of you look like that picture and the last time this happened the..."

"The last time?" Interrupted Arowan.

"Yes, when I drew a dragon and ended up in a world of half dragon, half human people."

There was the briefest hush and then another torrent of questions. The dark eel creature forgotten for now.

Mouse spent the rest of the evening telling her story about

her adventure. About the evil Kromus and the kind Zable and all her friends she'd shared some time with. She told her new friends about the reason for her going there, about hiding in the mountains and being kidnapped, albeit briefly, by Kromus. They all sat with big wide eyes when she told them about Zable and the battles, to the death, in some cases.

When she finished, by telling them that she must have fallen asleep because she woke up back under her tree in her village, several mouths were agape!

"Wow." Said Angel.

"I just loved being with them and I just hope that their world is now peaceful."

"I can't believe you stabbed one!" Exclaimed Angel.

Mouse giggled, "Me either."

Mouse answered nearly a million more questions about her previous adventure before stifling a yawn.

Arowan stood up and announced that it was late and they had all better get their last swim in before going to sleep.

"You must be tired Mouse?" He asked.

"Actually I am a bit sleepy but I have had a wonderful evening, thankyou everyone." She looked around at the many faces around her and she noticed something other than curiosity, the warmth in their eyes was still present but she noticed something else – respect.

As Mouse lay next to Angel, who was wrapped in her moist cover on the hard rock bed, she thought about her day in this new place. She was accustomed to danger, surprises and meeting 'not entirely human' friends, so she came to the conclusion that apart from the beast who tried to consume her, it had been quite a good day.

She snuggled into the nearly soft blanket that one of the

33

women villagers had hastily woven for her out of a dry cottony twine and the only recurring thought she had was what on earth had she been sent here for?

*

While Bichir was in a calm and peaceful state, ripples appeared on the surface of the pool. Several pairs of beady, black eyes emerged and scanned the lagoon. Without so much as a small splash the intruders moved about in the water unnoticed and silent.

Not wanting to be spotted, the long, sleek bodies slithered around the pool for a few minutes before retreating back into the watery tunnel, and back to the ocean.

***

Chapter Three

Mouse awoke to strange unfamiliar noises and smells. As she opened her eyes and remembered where she was, she looked over the bed to find Angel had already got up and gone.

She stretched and heard a weird squeaky sound as she did so, and it seemed to be coming from the costume she was wearing. It was almost as if the garment had dried out and groaned a bit as she stretched it! Mouse looked around the cave, the curtain of long leafy branches pulled back once again to reveal shafts of brilliant sunshine.

Mouse made her way to the front of the dwelling and peeped outside. She was spotted.

"Mouse, come." Said Arowan.

Mouse joined the family of four as they sat in a group eating some fruit for breakfast. Arowan handed her a bowl.

"We weren't sure what you liked to eat for breakfast, so after our morning swim, we all gathered some berries for you?" Said Angel's younger sister, Trahira.

"That's kind, thankyou." Mouse smiled.

"And after eating I thought I could show Mouse where we fish, out in the ocean?" Suggested Angel.

"That's ok with me as long as Mouse can swim Angel?" Both looked at Mouse.

"Yes I can swim, I have won competitions at school for front crawl!" Announced Mouse proudly but realised that Arowan and Angel had no idea what that meant so she just repeated, "I can swim very well."

"Cool, we'll finish eating and then head off." Said Angel.

"Are you going with Bonito, Tang, Vimba and Mora?" Asked Arowan.

"Of course dad," replied Angel, "safety in numbers and all that!" Angel rolled her eyes at her dad.

"And make sure your pouches are full."

"Yes dad." Angel looked at Mouse, "Come on Mouse, let's get ready to go." And with that she leapt to her feet, grabbed Mouse's hand and pulled her back to her dwelling.

Once back in the dwelling Mouse asked "What pouches need to be full and what do they need to be full of?"

"Oh, just our stem pouches."

"I don't understand what that is?"

"Right, ok, we have to eat the stem of a special plant grown in the volcanic spring when we go swimming in the ocean to allow us to breathe underwater."

"Breathe under water?" Mouse repeated and Angel saw the confused look on Mouse's face. She took her hand and sat her down on the hard, rocky bed, while she gathered various tools and weapons for fishing and explained about the pouches.

"At the back of the beach here in Bichir is a hidden cave where a special plant grows in the volcanic spring water. We pick it and eat it just before we get to the ocean, so that we have more time underwater to fish."

"Wow, that's so cool!" Exclaimed Mouse.

"Come on, I'll show you and you'll see what I mean."

Angel gathered her small spears, knives and nets and attached them to her costume on little loops that Mouse hadn't noticed before, and headed out the cave. Mouse followed her until they were both standing in front of the leafy covered rock face.

"I don't see anything?" Queried Mouse.

"Follow me."

Angel stepped three or four paces to the right of where they had been standing, and to Mouse's surprise, what had looked like a solid rock face was in fact two layers of rock which overlapped each other leaving a small gap between the layers, just enough to squeeze through.

Mouse followed Angel through the tight gap, pulling aside the vegetation which had cleverly concealed its existence. She found herself in an almost identical version of Bichir but in miniature. The pool of water was crystal clear and you could see that the bottom was covered in the plant Angel had been talking about. And every so often an echoey 'plop' bounced around the chamber.

"Where does that water come from Angel?" Said Mouse as she located the source of the 'plop'.

"That drip is from an underground volcanic spring deep within the volcano." She said, "As it flows through the various levels of rock, on its way here, it picks up a specific mineral which gives this plant its magical power."

As Mouse looked down into the clear shallow water at the

extremely nondescript plant, she wondered if the plant would have the same effect on her.

She watched Angel produce a small leathery pouch, bend down to the water's edge and pick a handful of the plant from the root and carefully put it in the pouch. She then placed that pouch into a secondary pouch and pulled the top tight with some twine.

"Why are there two pouches?"

"It's just a double layer to protect the plant from the salt water in the sea."

"Does the salt kill it?"

"Not really but it just stays 'fresher' the longer the salt water doesn't get to it."

Mouse finally voiced her thoughts, "Do you think it will work for me too?"

Angel stopped fiddling with the pouch and fishing tools and looked at Mouse.

"Only one way to find out!" She smiled.

Happy that she had everything she needed for their little trip to the sea, Angel checked that the pouch was securely attached to her costume, took Mouse by the hand and they both squeezed back through the gap in the rock face and headed across the beach.

They made their way toward the tunnel that the men had come through yesterday after going fishing, and there, waiting waist deep in water were Angel's friends.

"Finally!" Said Tang.

"Come on slow coaches, we've been waiting ages." Laughed Vimba.

Mouse and Angel jumped into the cool refreshing water and made their way towards the tunnel. Angel had nearly disappeared from view when she realised that Mouse wasn't behind her.

Mouse could hear Tang say "Doesn't look like Mouse wants to come after all!"

Angel turned back to find Mouse at the mouth of the tunnel.

"It looks cold, dark and wet in there?" She said to Angel.

"It isn't pleasant, I'll admit, but if you hold onto me I'll guide you through. We're not in the tunnel for very long."

"Where does it lead to?"

"It leads out to the river, which then runs into the sea."

"Oh." Was all Mouse could manage.

"It's ok Mouse, it's only half filled with water so you can still swim normally and it's just fresh water."

"Does it take long to get to the river?"

"Not really, five minutes or so." Angel put her arm around Mouse, "C'mon, I'll keep hold of you."

Angel led Mouse to the tunnel and slowly they disappeared from Bichir.

It was cool in the tunnel, and true to her word, Angel held onto Mouse for the short swim in the dark. Before long they were out the other side and swimming along in the bright sunshine.

The river was narrow and lined on both banks with the same jungle like trees and plants. As Mouse swam she kept a keen eye on the riverbanks for any snarling, hungry beasts.

Thankfully she saw none.

As the water started to get murkier and the taste of salt became apparent Angel and her friends swam to the edge of the river, and hauled themselves up onto a rocky platform.

Mouse followed.

"This is the best place to eat the Oxystemla." Announced Angel, pulling out some of the plant from the doubly protected pouches.

"How long will that little bit last Angel?" Mouse asked as Angel placed a small amount of the plant into her mouth.

"This will allow us just over an hour or so." Replied Angel, "Here, have a little bit and let's see what happens."

Mouse took the small wet plant from Angel, sniffed at it and then put it in her mouth.

"Just chew it in your mouth for a minute or two and then swallow it." Explained Vimba.

Mouse was quite surprised that the taste wasn't too bad, "It tastes a bit like metal would taste but sweeter." She grinned.

The others all laughed, "That metal taste is the mineral that gets into our bloodstream to oxygenate our blood." Said Bonito.

"I don't feel any different though?"

"You won't," said Angel, "but you will have to test it here first before we go out into the ocean."

"How?"

"Take a deep breath and put your head under water, slowly let out your breath... and wait."

"Wait for what exactly?" Mouse wasn't entirely sure about this.

"See how long you can stay under." Sneered Tang, "If you need to come up for air then just lift your head. It's not rocket science."

"Shut up Tang. Mouse has never done this before." Snapped Bonito.

They all plopped back into the water.

All eyes were on Mouse as she summoned up the courage

to dunk her head under the water. She took a deep breath and disappeared.

She exhaled slowly and waited.

And waited.

She was soon joined underwater by five heart shaped, smiley faces.

"It worked for you too!" Screeched Angel.

"Did it? How long have I been under water?"

"Long enough to know that it worked. Now come on, we're wasting time!" And with that Tang pushed off from the rock into the river and was soon out of sight in the gloomy river.

The others rolled their eyes and then too, pushed off from the rock, into the river, and headed towards the sea.

A bit bewildered, Mouse copied them and had soon caught up with the others. She discovered that she could swim a lot faster under the water and was easily able to keep up.

It wasn't long before the open sea was in sight, and the river's water cleared as it mingled with the turquoise blue of the ocean.

Mouse rested in the shallows for a moment, amongst the fishing gear which had been casually tossed aside, and watched Angel and her friends frolicking about in the sea. They threw each other about, dived and performed hand stands; long legs waving around in the air.

Bored of just watching, and breath caught, Mouse swam out to where they were and joined in. She was being pushed high into the air for the fourth time when she noticed a shadow in the water, not far away, which stopped her heart!

She was launched, she splashed into the sea and she screamed, as she waded as fast as she could back to the shore.

"What is it Mouse?" Angel cried after her, as she saw terror in Mouse's eyes.

"I-I-I saw a fin Angel!" Spluttered Mouse, "Get everyone out of the water, there's a shark coming this way!"

Angel looked out to the horizon and then at all her friends, who were all now looking in the same direction.

"There!" Pointed Mouse, "There it is!"

The five friends looked at each other, turned to Mouse and all burst out laughing.

"Mouse," said Angel, "Mouse, look." She pointed at the sea and at that very moment a dolphin emerged and deftly balanced on its tail as he moved towards them all.

"Oh ...." Sighed Mouse, "I just saw a fin and panicked." She mustered up a weak smile.

"Come on Mouse, come and meet Torpedo."

"Is it friendly then?"

"Of course – watch."

With that Mouse watched as Vimba was hurled into the air at considerable speed off the nose of Torpedo. She literally flew through the air, executed the most perfect somersault before diving back into the water without making so much as a plop!

Mouse edged her way back to the deeper water where the others were now taking turns to be tossed into the air. She had never seen a dolphin before, only on the television, and she was going to make the most of it.

Keeping her eyes firmly fixed on the dolphin, she got closer, but would she be brave enough to get as close as the others, she wasn't sure.

Something brushed past her leg.

Something that was dark and quite large.

"Angel!" She shouted.

"Oh my goodness, what could it be this time?" Teased Tang.

Angel shot an annoyed look at Tang and swam over to Mouse. "What is it, are you ok?"

"Something brushed past my leg." Whispered Mouse so the others couldn't hear. Mouse was extremely aware that she sounded like a small child, frightened of everything.

"What did it look like?"

"I only saw it for a second but it was quite big and possibly round."

"Round?" Echoed Angel.

"Don't fret Mouse, I think it was probably Discus, a turtle who swims with Torpedo."

"A turtle?"

"Yeah, they swim along this coastline together, all around the island sometimes. We haven't seen them for days but they must know it's a special day and have come to see you!"

Mouse was amazed – seeing a dolphin for the first time was utterly incredible, but to see a turtle for the first time, on the same day, was unbelievable.

"They won't hurt you Mouse," said Angel, "they just play with us for a while and then go on their way."

"Oh, ok." Said Mouse, but Angel didn't hear her as she turned away and dove into the water to join the others who were happily messing about with the dolphin and the turtle.

Mouse decided that this would probably never happen again so she snapped out of her fearful state and swam over to the others. The six of them played with Torpedo and Discus for a while; taking it in turns to be pushed

43

along by Torpedo's nose and holding onto the shell of Discus while diving up and down and in and out of the coral at the bottom of the sea. Mouse had a great time in the cool water and feeling the hot sun on her face as she got thrown about with the others. After a while two things happened; Torpedo and Discus decided enough was enough and headed off, and Angel produced some more Oxystemla for them before they ventured into deeper water to do some fishing.

They gathered up the tools which were left scattered about in the shallow water and then swam out to sea.

It wasn't long before everyone had caught something, except Mouse. Angel tried to help her but they had no luck.

"I'm not great at this but let's move into the thicker coral where there are more fish and it may be easier to catch one or two." Suggested Angel.

The two girls, topped up with the magical little plant, swam out deep into the denser part of the coral reef where the fish were definitely more plentiful. Mouse and Angel watched, for a moment, as colourful blurs of colour darted in and out of the various shapes and sizes of swaying coral. Angel then moved behind Mouse to help hold her small spear, and held her almost motionless except for their long hair which danced slowly, to and fro, like thin silvery seaweed.

Slowly Angel lifted Mouse's arm, higher and higher, until it was behind her back in a striking position. Both girls had spotted the shoal of large yellow fish just drifting carelessly in and out of the coral only inches away.

"Ready?" Angel whispered in Mouse's ear.

But before they could strike their targets, the whole shoal

darted off at great speed.

"Where did they go?" Asked Mouse.

"Ssshhh." Whispered Angel as she lowered Mouse's arm and took her spear from her.

Both girls' heads snapped round as a flash of black and orange whizzed past them, right where the shoal of fish had been, only moments before.

"What was that?" Muttered Mouse, certain that it wasn't another one of Angel's friendly sea creatures.

"I think it was one of the Queen's serpents."

And before Mouse could respond with yet another question, the water shifted as the black and orange creature sped past them once again.

"Come on Mouse." Angel grabbed her hand.

They started to swim for the open sea where the others were but didn't get very far before the serpent appeared from behind them and just stopped and floated in front of them.

Every time Mouse and Angel made a move it blocked their way, and then just floated in front of them again.

A menacing, long bodied snake like creature with sharp spines on its head and down its back. It's black and orange face only a few feet away from them, and it's mainly black body, with patterns in stark white, curving and writhing behind it.

It did nothing.

It said nothing.

Angel and Mouse gripped each other tightly but daren't move. Mouse could feel the water shifting again, even though none of them were moving a muscle.

The serpent was joined by three more of its kind. Mouse could tell by Angels tightening grip that this situation wasn't good.

Angel and Mouse could only watch as the first serpent remained in the same spot whilst the newcomers weaved in circular movements around it, like a swirling mass of ugly eels.

The first one was definitely bigger than the other three and he was definitely the most evil looking one of the four.

Angel and Mouse clung to each other tighter than ever as the smaller serpents slowly moved away from the larger one and began to weave their way closer to where they were, suspended in petrified stillness.

The three serpents squirmed their way around their legs, their bodies and up to their faces. When the smaller ones opened their mouths with a hissing noise, close to the girls' faces, they revealed rows of small sharp pointy teeth, not dissimilar to Angels.

The serpent's mouths stayed open and they hissed once again.

The larger serpent slowly and deliberately pushed his big black and orange head to the front of the writhing throng.

"Inanya!" He spat.

And in an instant, they were gone.

Mouse and Angel didn't let go of each other straight away but did allow their bodies to relax somewhat as the tension of the last few minutes lessened.

"Have they gone?" Whispered Mouse.

"I think so." Said Angel as she whipped her head around in all directions checking for the serpents, "Let's get back to the others."

The girls separated and swam as fast as they could to join the others. Angel quickly told them all what had happened and the decision was made to return to Bichir immediately.

The journey back was frantic so it took them no time at all, Mouse wasn't even worried about going back through the tunnel.

Once through, and safely on the beachy area in Bichir, Angel searched for her dad.

Arowan heard the commotion as the six of them excitedly told the tale to the first villagers they came across once emerging from the tunnel, so he found them before they came looking for him.

"Ok, ok. Calm down." He said as he tried to hush the crowd which had now formed around the six youngsters. He looked at Angel.

"What happened to sticking together young lady, I thought I could trust you?"

"We were all together for most of the time but I took Mouse to the reef to fish because we weren't catching anything." She bowed her head, knowing full well her dad was furious.

Mouse didn't know where to look, or what to say.

"You know you should never go off like that. Those serpents wouldn't have come anywhere near the six of you but just you and Mouse – you were lucky they let you go unharmed."

"But they just looked at us dad, nothing else." Explained Angel.

"That's it? They didn't touch you at all?"

"That's all." Angel shot Mouse 'a look' which she didn't understand the meaning of.

"They just said Inanya and then left." Mumbled Mouse.

The meaning of Angel's look became apparent very quickly.

The entire crowd, by now most of the villagers, started

talking at once and as Mouse looked at Arowan his face was thunderous.

"And were *you* going to tell me about that Angel?" He spat.

"I didn't want to worry you." She whispered.

"It's bad enough that *she* now knows about Mouse but to come back here and not tell me so that we can be prepared for whatever may happen next is unbelievable!"

"I'm sorry dad."

"Ok, ok, well at least we know now," he looked around at everyone gathered at the beach, "we must all be extra vigilant and only go fishing in groups. And no matter what, you must not go anywhere alone."

The villagers all nodded their white haired heads and mumbled their agreement.

Arowan turned to Mouse and said, "I think we owe you an explanation, you look scared half to death."

"I'm ok," muttered Mouse, "I just haven't got a clue what's going on and what I have to do with it."

"We all need to take a swim, refresh ourselves and this afternoon we will gather again and explain the whole thing to you."

"Ok," said Mouse, "that sounds good to me."

With that the villagers dispersed in various directions and left Arowan with the six friends.

"Tell me exactly what happened." He said.

Angel told him about messing about with Torpedo and Discus, then doing a bit of unsuccessful fishing, then onto their encounter with the serpents.

"And where on the reef were you?"

"Only on the edge of the reef, where the shoals of fish go and the coral is a bit more dense."

"You didn't go any further than that?" Arowan looked at both Angel and Mouse.

Both girls shook their heads.

"Ok," Arowan turned to the others, "go and take a dip to get rid of the salt water and we'll see you a bit later."

Obediently Tang, Vimba, Bonito and Mora shuffled off.

Arowan, Mouse and Angel stood still and stayed silent for a moment, each wrapped up in their own thoughts.

"Why don't you get Mouse's clothes and rinse them in the pool so they are clean, then they can dry out?" Suggested Arowan.

Both girls nodded and made their way to Angels' dwelling. Mouse scooped up her clothes and looked at Angel, "I'm so sorry I got you into trouble Angel."

"Oh it's ok, it's not your fault, I should have told him myself."

"Do you think we can forget about it for a while and go for a nice swim in the pool?"

"Sure, let's get your clothes washed and hung up to dry and have a muck about with the others."

Tang, Vimba, Bonito and Mora were already in the pool and after Mouse and Angel had sloshed the clothes about a bit and thrown them over some rocks in the sun, they joined in the fun.

The morning's events forgotten for a while, they swam, they splashed and they dunked each other. Mouse felt 'accepted' by all of Angel's friends, all except one – Tang – but she couldn't work out why.

After an hour or so the villagers began to gather, food was being prepared and everyone felt drawn to the beach area for the afternoon.

In a dark underwater cave in the middle of the coral reef a long, black spiny tail was whipping back and forth in the water. All around the cave was a frenzy of black and orange serpents, all desperate to hear Inanya's plans involving the human girl. The larger serpent approached her and asked, "Are you thinking what I'm thinking?"
Inanya turned her head towards him, her sleek black hair swaying in the water, and nodded.
And together they whispered, "The Trident."

*

Arowan sat on a large boulder which lay up against the rock face, looking out over the sea of faces who were all eager for him to start the story. They all knew the tale, and knew this was for Mouse's benefit, but they never tired of hearing it.
"Ok everyone, I think it's time to explain to our new friend, our history; how we became who we are and how Inanya became who she is."
Murmurs in the 'audience' signalled their approval.
"So I'll begin....

Hundreds of years ago, possibly thousands, this island did not exist. The three pointed volcano that you see today was in fact under the sea, rumbling and erupting every decade or so.
We also didn't exist as we are today, the underwater volcano was pitted with many caves, and in these caves lived the mer-people. They lived solely under the water and lived in family groups. They were half human half fish creatures with beautiful turquoise shimmering tails. The mer-men were darker in colour

with much stronger upper bodies and their tails were thicker and more muscular than those of the mer-maids. They hunted, they fought when necessary and protected their families no matter what.

The mer-maids were more slender, wore their hair long, their tails much more willowy than the mer-men and they were the ones who nurtured the young and taught them the mer-people ways.

The villages were always ruled by a king or queen of the mer-people and for many years lived harmoniously in this way. That is until one family committed an awful crime against the current king and he sought revenge. At the time there were several families living in caves quite close to the royal residence, but the caves were quite obviously much smaller in comparison and far less grand. All, bar one family, accepted this as natural, after all he was the king! He would be the one to have the larger cave decorated with jewels and treasures, as had all the kings and queens before him. This king lived and reigned peacefully with his chosen mer-maid and their two daughters.

One day, the dissatisfied family, who were ancient ancestors of Inanya, decided that the king and queen should be taught a lesson, and the lesson was that they should all be equal. The family began to plot ways to cause problems for the king. At first they were mischievous and snuck into the king's cave and moved things around but they soon tired of these trivial activities which weren't really affecting the king at all.

One evening all the families gathered together to listen to the king's report, as they did every week or so. The mer-people came together and waited for the king to arrive, looking upwards at the throne on the stone platform carved out of the rock, which was close to the king's cave. He would walk, as he did every time, from his residence along the platform and into a cave which was

51

positioned behind the throne called The Cave of Thrones. This cave was heavily guarded at all times as this was the place where The Trident was hidden and all the king's treasures and jewels were kept. He would then appear from behind the throne itself and hold up his arms to his people. There would be cheering and excited cries from the mer-people below as he waved The Trident aloft, for all to see.

However, on this occasion, when the king emerged, placed the royal Trident at the head of the throne and sat down to address the people, there was one group of mer-people who were not cheering and waving.

The king started talking to his people but one family weren't listening, their eyes firmly fixed on the bejewelled Trident which, when placed in the throne, mirrored the three points of the volcano which could be seen in the distance behind the throne.

Without uttering a word to each other, the father, mother and two sons knew exactly what they were going to do. So over the next few days the family watched the movements of the king, the queen and the princesses and hatched a plan to steal The Trident. The greedy family didn't consider the consequences of the crime they were about to commit, nor did they consider what would happen if their plan went wrong.

Impatient and selfish, the family decided they couldn't wait any longer. That day would be the day that the two sons would distract the princesses whilst they would visit the Cave of Thrones to steal The Trident and anything else they could get their thieving hands on. With The Trident in their possession, they would be able to demand a more equal existence.

The plan was underway.

The whole family watched the king's cave for an hour or so and saw the king and queen leave for their daily rounds where they visited their people, checked the security nets – something they did themselves every day – and then took themselves off for a leisurely swim around volcano summit near to the surface of the water to revel in the sunshine.

The mother, a beautiful but vain creature, approached the guards at the entrance to The Cave of Thrones and flirted shamelessly with the guards and distracted them enough for her husband to slip quickly into the treasure filled cave.

So far, so good.

Meanwhile, the two sons had found the princesses gathering shells on the sea bed, in a small coral reef, near to the king's cave, their guardians not far away. As the boys approached the girls, the guards immediately swam over to protect the royal princesses.

But the boys were sly, so with one eye on their parents and seeing their father slip past one set of guards, they carried on with their plan. They had already been gathering shells of their own and showed the girl's protectors, explaining that they were just gifts and wanted to help the princesses with their collecting.

The two princesses, glad of the male company, assured the guards that they would be ok and they would stay close by.

Satisfied that the boys had no weapons on them, the guards agreed to let them help the girls, and left the four young mer-people to carry on collecting the colourful shells from the sea bed.

What the guards couldn't possibly know, is what would happen next.

The boys charmed the girls with their playful antics and enticing behaviour and slowly but surely, were leading them further and further away from the safety of the caves, the village and their guards.

Before long they were up against the security netting which was cleverly woven between various growths of coral. The girls were suddenly quite aware of how unprotected they were but the *devious boys comforted them and re-assured them that they were safe.*

The four of them were swimming up and down the lengths of the nets when one of the boys shouted out "Wow! Look at that shell." The other boy joined in the excited waving and pointing even though they knew the shell would be there because that's where they had left it the day before.

The princesses swam up to the net and looked to where the boys were indicating and sure enough there sat the biggest and most colourful shell either of them had ever seen! It didn't occur to them that it was oddly placed in clear view, on its' own, with no similar shells nearby.

The boys started to pull on the net to see if they could get through; yet another remarkable performance because they had already cut a hole in the net and pulled the rest of the net down, snagging it on some coral so that no one would see it.

The girls whispered together, debating whether or not the risk was worth the shell.

The shell won.

The boys acted out their scene perfectly and revealed the supposed tear in the netting. They all swam through, and straight to the shell.

The boys, pleased with themselves, having given their parents enough time to get The Trident, but not too long so as the princesses would be missed. Time to get back.

They watched the girls both holding the large shell, turning it round and round to see all the colours and curves, their faces almost illuminated by the pleasure of owning such a shell.

Unfortunately, as they were turning it over and over, it slipped from their hands and back down on to the sea bed. The older princess giggled and swam down to pick it up.

But at that moment, the younger princess was left alone,

suspended in the deep water. She didn't stand a chance against the huge monstrous shark like creature as it sped towards her from nowhere. It opened its mouth, lined with large jagged teeth, top and bottom, caught her in his jaws and disappeared with her as quickly as he had appeared!

There was an almighty scream from the older princess as she looked at the two boys who's mouths were wide open in utter disbelief.

This was the beginning of the end for the greedy family as not one of their plans had been successful.

The next events were the result of their crimes.

The parents had not found the Trident, let alone been able to steal it. So they had returned to their cave empty handed all except for some small treasures.

The guards had returned and had to explain to the unsuspecting king and queen that they had lost their daughters.

The older princess had swum home as fast as she could not giving the boys a second thought. Several other guards tried to intercept her but all she could mutter was "I want my dad."

The days that followed were mournful and quiet, all the volcano's people were in shock.

But then came the king's fury.

The princess was finally able to identify the boys, the parents too, identified by the guards of The Cave of Thrones. The story unravelled.

The family were brought before the king and queen, ironically in The Cave of Thrones, where the king, Trident in his hand, asked them "Why?"

Heads bowed, the family of four didn't even offer an explanation.

So, revenge at the forefront of his mind, the king pointed The Trident at them and cursed the whole family to a life of darkness and misery.

The four, once beautiful mer-people, were instantly transformed into grey bodied, black tailed, slippery creatures. The shape of their bodies being the only thing that resembled what they used to be. The colourless family were destined never to leave the depths of the ocean and never to feel the sun on their faces again.

They swam away, past the edge of the volcano, past the nets and into the deep, dark sea.

The king was feeling a little better but he hadn't finished yet!

Next he summoned the guards, and their families, who had meant to have been looking after The Cave of Thrones and his two precious daughters.

At least this rabble had the decency to plead their apologies thought the king as he once again pointed the Trident at the sorrowful crowd.

He was in no mood for pity, or excuses.

The once colourful mer-people suffered a much more severe transformation than the pathetic, greedy family. He had entrusted his greatest treasures, his daughters firstly and then his bejewelled possessions so he felt their crimes were far more treacherous.

The punishment should, therefore, fit the crime.

The guards and their families were transformed into serpents; long bodied, spiny, dark slippery serpents.

So with one last look at their old life, the newly transformed serpents slithered off into the depths of the sea, banished from ever coming anywhere near the volcano again.

The king and his queen had to live with the sorrow of losing their daughter for the rest of their lives but were still able to rule with courage and kindness.

Now ... that happened hundreds and hundreds of years ago and many kings and queens have come and gone since then. But there was far more to happen in our history than the making of

Inanya's ancestors.

Not long after those events took place, the volcano, which used to just rumble every decade, decided it was time for a change and so it erupted. The force of such a huge eruption forced the volcano above sea level and burning hot lava spilled down its' sides which cooled as it hit the water to form flatlands, and the many tunnels that weave their way through and around the island.

Over the centuries that followed there have been many eruptions and more and more of the volcano has surfaced to become the island we have today. You can still make out the three peaks if you can get a clear view of the volcano's summit.

But that is not all.

Over the centuries, the mer-people have been divided. There are those that still live 100% in the sea and then there are those who have evolved gradually, to be able to live on land.

As for the Trident, well that remains a bit of a mystery. It is believed to be hidden away, still, in The Cave of Thrones. But as that cave is now halfway up the volcano, above the sea, no one has ever been able to discover whether or not it really is there.

Arowan looked around at all the familiar faces and then to Mouse.

"So there you have it Mouse, our history in a condensed version. Of course there have been battles and royal troubles throughout, but that particular event explains how Inanya's ancestors came to be and how she is today; the result of a greedy, selfish family who paid the price for their crime, and have done ever since."

"It's amazing to think all that happened so long ago but it still affects all of you, even now." Said Mouse to the remaining villagers who hadn't slipped off for a swim.

"I'd be lying if I told you I wasn't worried that Inanya is

out to cause trouble." Frowned Arowan.

"What sort of trouble Arowan?"

"Well, we haven't had any problems with her for a few years..." his eyes met Angels and Mouse noticed a sadness and understanding in both pairs of big eyes, "but on the whole, we don't have much to do with her."

"And now, because of me, there might be more trouble?"

"Possibly, but we'll all be extra careful from now on," Arowan smiled at Mouse, "we'll be ok Mouse so please don't worry."

"It's a little hard not to, after what happened with the dragons." Mumbled Mouse.

"I know, and you must have been very scared, but you were brave, and got home in one piece."

"Yes, I know but I knew what they needed me for. I have no idea why I'm here, or if anyone knows how to get me home."

Arowan gave her a fatherly squeeze, "It'll be ok, I promise. I will do my best to keep us all safe and find out how to get you home."

Angel smiled a sad smile at her dad, took Mouse's hand and went for a late afternoon swim.

***

Chapter Four

That evening was spent in much the same way as the previous evening; a gathering on the beach, food, conversations and regular dips in the lagoon. The only noticeable difference was the lack of laughter.

By the time Mouse and Angel went to sleep, they were exhausted and ready for a rest, after the events of the day had taken its toll.

*

Inanya had been busy making plans. She had realised, along with her serpents, that Mouse could be the answer to all their prayers, and at last there was someone on the island who could search for The Trident. She was the only one who didn't need to be near water all the time. She was the only one who could venture into the hidden caves of the volcano. She was the only one who could find The

Trident and finally lift the curse of hundreds of years ago. Inanya would be turned back into a beautiful mermaid, her serpents, who were also her only family, and her guardians would all be returned to who they should be. And having spent centuries skulking around in dark and murky waters all their lives, would all enjoy the warmth of the sun on their faces once again.

*

As Mouse sat on the beach area in Bichir eating fruit and feeling the sun streaming down on her, Angel was trying to convince her to go back out to the ocean once again.

"There'll be lots of us this time, and we'll all stick together, so nothing can happen." Pleaded Angel.

Mouse looked at Angel's pretty face doubtfully.

"If I could be sure that we'd all be safe, it would be great, I loved messing about yesterday with Torpedo, Discus and you guys but..."

Mouse was uncertain about what could happen and wondered if Arowan had indeed known what trouble she could bring to their doorstep.

"I promise we'll stay together – loads of us?" Angel didn't give up easily it seemed.

She grabbed Mouse's hand and bounced up and down excitedly, "Pleeease?" She pleaded.

"I don't know."

"Mouse, it'll be ok, I'll get everyone to come, and we'll see if Torpedo and Discus are about too?"

Angel's excitement was infectious so Mouse felt she had no choice in the matter.

"Ok, ok. If it'll stop you bouncing up and down like an

idiot!" She laughed.

"Hooray! I'll go and make sure the others are ready." And happily she skipped off, on her great long legs, the sunlight catching the colours of the small fin on her back.

Within minutes Mouse was surrounded by 'the gang' and they were all ready to go. Each had their collection of fishing tools which consisted of small spears and knives, hooks and netting.

"Right, are we good to go?" Asked Angel.

"All except for the Oxystemla." Replied Vimba.

"Right. You wait here Mouse, and we'll go and get some and be back in a minute." And off they went, leaving Mouse alone again.

Arowan noticed she was on her own and walked over to where she was sat.

"Are you ok Mouse? Why are you sat here on your own? Where are the others?"

Mouse explained where they were and outlined their plans for the day.

"And how do you actually feel about going back out to the ocean?" He asked knowingly.

Mouse smiled, "I'm a little worried about seeing a serpent again but we're all going to stick together properly this time so hopefully they'll stay away from us."

"I hope so, but if you see anything unusual at all, you all come straight back to Bichir."

Mouse giggled.

Arowan frowned.

"I'm sorry Arowan but nearly everything I see here is unusual to me!"

Arowan understood and laughed too, "Yes, I suppose it is. Ok, let me re-phrase that. Keep an eye out for anything that is unusual for here."

"Deal."

Angel and her friends returned to the beach but stopped in their tracks when they saw Arowan sat next to Mouse, with his hand on her shoulder.

"Dad?"

"Angel, I was just explaining to Mouse that you must all return to Bichir immediately if you see anything unusual."

"Of course we will, won't we?" Four heads nodded in agreement.

"Well, hopefully you will all just have some fun today. Be careful and I'll see you later."

Angel gave Arowan a kiss, grabbed Mouse's hands for the second time that morning, and they headed off into the tunnel.

Having stopped at the rock in the river to eat the Oxystemla, the group of friends reached the sea, much quicker than the day before, even though there was some trepidation about getting there.

To Mouse the water looked unreal, she still couldn't quite get over the clarity and colour of the water. And the beautiful shade of blue in the sky took her breath away.

Mouse stood in the shallows for a moment gazing out to the horizon which was calm and still.

The serenity was shattered the moment Torpedo shot out of the water, made the perfect arc, before disappearing once again into the ocean. A torrent of whoops and cheers followed, as one by one, Angel's friends were hurled into the air off the end of Torpedo's nose.

Not being able to stand and watch any longer, Mouse swam out to join in the fun.

They took it in turns, just like the day before, playing with the dolphin, and when Discus appeared, he was also used as a plaything for the group of friends.

It was whilst Mouse was being pulled along by Discus that she spotted the flick of a shimmering, turquoise tail breaking the surface of the water.

This was quickly followed by a succession of more flicking tails.

Trying not to panic, she let Discus pull her back to where the others were still playing with Torpedo. Angel was in deep conversation with someone she hadn't met before, the owner of one of the flicking tails.

"Mouse! Mouse!" Angel shouted as she beckoned her over.

As Mouse got closer to them, she saw that the newcomer was very different to Angel and all the villagers of Bichir.

From what she could see, above water, the girl's hair was not the same bleached white as the villagers but more of a light caramel colour. Her eyes were as large as Angel's but not the clear blue, they were a deep green. And her skin, although still pale, instead of being a normal fleshy colour, had a slightly aquatic tone to it.

"Mouse, this is Salia. Salia this is Mouse, " Angel introduced them, "Salia belongs to one of the local mer-people villages, not far from here."

Mouse looked at Angel, looked at Salia and then disappeared under the water.

She surfaced moments later with a joyful grin all over her wet face.

"A *real* mer-maid! Just like the picture I drew first!" She gasped.

Angel and Salia giggled, "Yes, I'm a real mer-maid Mouse. Do you want to come and meet some more mer-people?"

"Oh, yes, can I?"

Angel signalled to the others and they all followed Salia a bit further around the coastline and then out to sea.

Angel pulled out her pouch of Oxystemla and the rest of the friends followed suit. Once 'topped up' they dove downwards to Salia's village.

It wasn't long before Mouse's eyes were as big and round as Angels. In all her childhood imaginings she had never pictured anything quite so magical.

Mer-maids, mer-men and youngsters were swimming all around her; tails glistening, hair billowing and bodies so graceful that she couldn't take her eyes off them.

"Beautiful aren't they?" Said Angel as she watched Mouse's reaction to the sight before them.

"I just can't believe how colourful and pretty they all are!"

Mouse suddenly realised she'd attracted some attention herself, something she was now getting used to. She answered questions, smiled and joked with the mer-people as they became aquainted.

Salia took Mouse by the hand and together they swam in and out of the seaweed, the coral and the small humps of seabed which were their homes. Angel followed them closely and she could understand Mouse's awe at these amazing people. Salia was laughing and swirling and pulling Mouse along with her. Mouse just didn't stop grinning from ear to ear! Salia was a princess of sorts, with her mum and dad being the leaders of this group of mer-people, and she was constantly getting into trouble for not obeying the thousand rules which came with being the leader's daughter. Salia was far too much of a free spirit to be bound by restrictions.

They swam with the youngsters who wanted to know all about Mouse's magic tree and about the dragons. It was a condensed version but Mouse watched as their already large eyes, got even larger, as the story unfolded.

Salia then took Mouse to meet her parents who were just as fascinated to meet a real human and plied her with questions about her world and how she got to Volmère. Mouse answered all their questions and asked some of her own, after all it wasn't every day that you got to meet leaders of a group of mer-people. Next she was whisked off to find Angel and the others for a game of hide and seek with the younger mer-people, which was not easy for Mouse as she was not familiar with the underwater terrain, and she was found first every time!

Soon it was time for Mouse and her friends from Bichir to head off to go fishing. So they bade their farewells and headed back the way they came but decided to steer clear of the coral reef, and instead, focus around some underwater caves were the larger fish dwelled. They all bobbed up to the surface for a few moments to eat some more Oxystemla, then swam back down to the caves where the seabed vegetation was tall and thick.

The six friends played amongst the tall seaweed for a while and then realised that if they didn't get some fishing done soon, they would all be in trouble with Arowan.

They all fanned out but stayed within sight of each-other and within minutes most of them had caught a large fish each.

All except Mouse.

"I just can't do it," she huffed, "I'm not quick enough."

Impatiently Tang swam over to where she was attempting to stalk a fish and grabbed the spear from her hand. The movement startled the fish and it swam away.

"You're never going to get the hang of this!" Snapped

Tang.

"I don't think so either." Giggled Mouse as she tried to lighten the atmosphere between them.

Tang just glared at her.

Mouse looked for Angel, who was concentrating on getting her catch into the netting, aided by Vimba.

She was about to join them, feeling a little mystified about Tangs attitude towards her when a large, cold hand clamped over her mouth and her entire body jerked as she was forced backwards into even denser seaweed.

Tang managed to shout for Angel before he too was forced backwards into the dark seaweed.

Four sets of eyes could only watch in horror as Mouse and Tang disappeared from sight!

They all darted, as quickly as they could, to where they had last seen them, searching in amongst the thick ribbons of vegetation.

"There!" Shouted Bonito as he pointed towards a cave entrance. Angel, Vimba and Mora all looked in the direction he was pointing just in time to see a long, dark, spiny tail slither into the dull light of the cave.

"Go and get help Mora," instructed Bonito, "the rest of us need to follow Mouse and Tang."

Mora set off as fast as she could, to get help from Salia and her villagers, whilst Bonito, Angel and Vimba cautiously made their way towards the cave.

Their approach did not go unnoticed for within moments they were surrounded by slippery serpents, hissing and glaring at them!

Every move they made to get past the evil looking serpents was mirrored, and they just could not get into the cave. The sleek black, white and orange bodies were just too

66

cunning for them.

"Mouse! Tang!" Shouted Angel.

No reply.

"What are we going to do?" She sighed.

*

The large clammy hand remained over Mouse's mouth and she could not get any leverage to bite into the slippery skin. She watched as Tang, with a face like thunder, was being unceremoniously bound in twine by several large serpents, one of which was the one she and Angel had encountered yesterday. He was not gagged and Mouse could not understand why he hadn't answered Angel when she had called their names.

The light in the cave was shadowy but as Mouse looked at Tang he just glared at her, without a word.

"You are, without a doubt, a most unexpected surprise my dear," a voice whispered in Mouse's ear from behind, "an absolute gift."

"What shall we do with him? The larger serpent asked as he nodded towards Tang.

"He hasn't shouted for help. I wonder why?"

"Perhaps he's clever enough to realise that it won't make any difference."

Mouse could feel Tang's eyes burning through to her soul but she could also see him wriggling about to try and free one of his arms. She had no idea why he hated her but she could only hope that he would be able to escape and get help. Her view of Tang was momentarily blocked as the large serpent swam up to her so they were face to face.

"A gift indeed my Queen." He spat and then he moved to

one side as Inanya showed herself at last.

Mouse still couldn't move the hand that was covering her mouth, but she didn't think she would have been able to utter a word anyway.

There, before her, was her transformed picture!

She had thought the paper version was horrific enough but this creature oozed evil. Inanya's eyes were as black as coal and her skin was a sallow grey colour, from the lack of sunlight all her life. Her long sleek hair seemed to have a life of its own as it moved about in the water, much like her very own serpents.

"I'm Inanya, the Serpent Queen, you may have heard about me from your little land loving friends and I ..." She was stopped mid sentence as the larger serpent let out an ear piercing wail!

It was the worse sound Mouse had ever heard, and as Inanya spun round to see what had happened, she was able to see Tang's small spear lodged in the back of the serpent.

Pre-occupied now, Inanya took her hand away from Mouse's mouth which heralded yet another scream.

This time from Mouse.

"Angel!" She shouted at the top of her voice.

She looked around for Tang but he had disappeared, but unfortunately all the noise had attracted many more serpents, as they came to assist their Queen.

The underwater cave was a writhing mass of serpents, all weaving in and out, not really knowing what to do, awaiting instruction from Inanya.

Mouse took the opportunity to make a dash for it.

She darted to the right of the Serpent Queen and shot towards the entrance of the cave. She came to an abrupt halt as she crashed head first into Bonito, who was swimming equally as fast into the cave!

And all they could hear from inside the cave was a shriek from Inanya, "GET HER!"

Mouse and Bonito recovered from their bump and started swimming away from the cave. But it wasn't long before they felt movement close behind them. Mouse could just see Angel up ahead and she had been joined by some of the mer-people, Torpedo and Discus.

Bonito, quite obviously, was a better swimmer than Mouse, so he grabbed her hand to pull her along. But just as he started to pull her forwards, she felt a sharp pain in her foot. As she dared to glance backwards, a serpent had his sharp teeth well and truly lodged around her ankle. She tried desperately to kick it free with her other foot but it wasn't budging.

Bonito soon realised that Mouse was all of a sudden a lot heavier to pull, he looked back and saw why.

They were nearing the others slowly but more and more serpents were gaining on them, and alone, Bonito knew that he wouldn't be able to keep hold of Mouse for much longer.

Staring straight ahead at the others, Bonito and Mouse struggled to get any nearer to them, but they were relieved to see the glint of spears in most hands.

All of a sudden , the group they were heading towards lurched forward, their spears outstretched in a war like advance.

Within seconds Torpedo had attacked the serpent who was still clinging on to Mouse's foot, his own sharp teeth sunk into the slimy flesh. The serpent instantly released Mouse, concern for it's own pain at the forefront of it's mind.

Bonito was able to surge forward with Mouse into the long seaweed, out of everyone's sight.

"Stay here Mouse. This has to be over quickly so we don't run out of Oxystemla." And with that he rushed back to help his friends.

Mouse, trembling from the attack of the serpent, watched from the safety of the seaweed curtain, knowing that this was one battle she wouldn't be able to help in. Her foot throbbed and was trailing blood with every kick of her legs.

So she did as she was told and stayed put.

She watched as Torpedo shook the serpent violently from side to side and then tossed it away as if done with it.

Discus was deftly circling another serpent, trying to stop it from joining in the fight but the slithery creature made a dash for it. Discus caught up with it just in time to clamp his powerful jaws around the serpent's tail. And although Discus wasn't strong enough or big enough to keep hold of the serpent, he managed to take a great big chunk out of it!

Meanwhile the mer-people and her friends were frantically jabbing spears at slippery bodies whenever they were in range.

It was a very disorganised fight.

And then Mouse saw her.

Through the mass of beautiful turquoise tails and the black and orange slimy ones, Inanya emerged from the cave. Her eyes were wide and horrified, as she took in the scene before her.

Mouse could see, even from where she was hiding, Inanya's eyes change into small, evil slits fuelled by anger. Mouse watched, unable to help, as Inanya chose a target, lunged forward, grabbed hold of some caramel coloured hair and sunk a small dagger into the stomach of one of the mer-maids!

The scream stopped everyone and everything in their tracks. All eyes on Inanya and her victim.

Inanya let go of the mer-maid as the water surrounding them was turning a deep red colour. And as the light faded from Salia's eyes, she drifted lifelessly to the sea bed.

Inanya spun round to face them all, a ghastly smile on her grey face.

"This is not over!" She shouted for all to hear, "this is only the beginning."

And with a whip of her long, spiny tail she and her serpents skulked off into the darker, deeper water, the injured serpents following slowly behind. The remaining bodies of two lay motionless just outside the entrance to the cave.

A moment of stillness ensued.

Then a rush of movement as everyone went to Salia.

Mouse came out of her hiding place and swam over to join everyone else. And as difficult as she found it to understand, she could actually see tears springing from the eyes of the mer-people; tears which formed and then just floated away in the gentle movement of the sea.

As everyone moved slowly around Salia, a sombre mood engulfed everyone. None more so than Mouse. Yet again she felt the weight of guilt on her young shoulders.

As one of the bigger mer-men lifted Salia's body from the ocean floor, all the mer-people gathered in close.

But the peace was shattered when Vimba shouted "Shark!"

All eyes swivelled around and saw what was heading towards them at a ridiculously rapid pace.

"It's the blood in the water!" Yelled Bonito, "get Salia into the seaweed, quickly, all of you!"

They didn't need telling twice.

Only Bonito remained in the open water. And his quick thinking sent him over to the two dead serpents where he used his knife to slit them open, and draw the ever nearing shark away from his friends.

The shark seemed confused for a moment, his enormous mouth agape, revealing rows of jagged lethal teeth. The lure of blood was a far greater temptation than the movement of the group, and he swerved, at the last second, towards the gutted serpents.

Bonito had managed to carry out the diversion and swim out of harm's way before the shark devoured one corpse in one mouthful.

As he rejoined the disbelieving group he said, "There'll be more very soon. Let's get away from here."

They all moved cautiously through the seaweed, all eyes on full alert, and could soon see Salia's village up ahead.

What they hadn't expected to see was Arowan in the middle of the village.

His face was set in an angry frown and his voice was thunderous as he tried to find out which direction Angel, Mouse and the rest of them had gone earlier that day.

The commotion of the returning villagers stopped him mid sentence and immediately his eyes softened as he saw Salia's lifeless body in the arms of one of her family.

He, and the villagers, went to them. Arowan's eyes now searching for Angel and Mouse. He saw them, finally, at the back of the group swimming together and holding hands. Both looked shaken up. He reached them intending to scream and shout at them but instead he pulled them together into a hug and said in a soft voice, "Let's just get home."

With no one really knowing what to say to each other, they bade their farewells and left the village and headed back to Bichir, leaving the mer-people to mourn silently for Salia.

No one had noticed that Tang was not with them.

*

Inanya was seething. She had been so close to capturing the human and keeping her for her own devious plans. She had spent the last few days plotting, since the arrival of Mouse, and even found a cave just above water to stash her until she had finalised her scheme.

Instead she was tending to the injuries of her wounded guardians, thanks to the surprising strength of the mer-people and the land lovers when they got together.

"You are angry my Queen, " said the largest serpent, "but if we are patient, we will have the girl."

"We were so close ..." Replied Inanya.

"They have to fish again soon."

"But I doubt they will bring her with them again."

"Maybe not, but they will send their strongest hunters to sea which leaves the poor human girl in Bichir virtually unprotected, and let's not forget our insider."

An evil toothy grin spread across Inanya's face.

"Excellent."

*

Bichir was bustling when they all emerged from the tunnel, and they were completely surrounded in seconds. Arowan instructed Angel, Mouse, Bonito and Vimba to go for a quiet swim after they had tended to their injuries, which thankfully, were superficial, whilst he tried to explain to the villagers what had happened. He wasn't sure he had heard the whole truth on the way home but it was enough to panic him to the core; memories of Inanya's greed and jealousy flooding back. If she could kill Angel's mother because of her beauty and grace, he knew she would stop at nothing to get Mouse.

For what, he hadn't yet worked out.

*

And when all was quiet once again, Tang slipped unnoticed into Bichir.

***

Chapter Five

That evening around the fire was a complete contrast to the previous two evenings, only the feast was the same. But whereas, before there had been merriment in the preparation, this night there was only movement.

Silence engulfed the lagoon.

Arowan stood on the edge of the beach watching his friends and his family going through the motions with fear on their faces.

He decided that he couldn't let this continue.

"Ok everyone!" He shouted, as all heads turned to look at him. "We've all been shocked by the events that took place today, and the tragedy of our friend Salia, but we must use tonight as a celebration of her. She would not want us all sad and quiet."

Several heads reluctantly nodded in agreement.

"Let's gather together, enjoy the food and bring our happy memories of Salia back to life."

So that's what they did.

And although the atmosphere was still a little heavy, the mood lifted and everyone took it in turns to tell stories about Salia, which brought smiles and the occasional laugh to Bichir.

*

Mouse awoke feeling something was wrong. When she was alert enough she realised that Angel's dwelling was shaking!

She sat bolt upright, threw her woven blanket off and looked at Angel, who had just felt the same thing.

"Angel?"

"I need to see my dad."

And with that, the two girls leapt of their rocky beds and went to find Arowan.

They weren't the only ones.

The whole lagoon was quivering and all the residents of Bichir looked alarmed.

Loose fragments of stones were spilling down the rock face like a sprinkling of sugar. The dangling vegetation which covered all the dwellings on the sides of Bichir, rustled against the cave walls.

Arowan climbed up to 'his' rock, carefully, and waved his arms to indicate silence.

"Everyone!" He shouted, "The volcano seems to have ˈwoken up but we must remain calm."

Unfortunately, calm was not how the people of Bichir were feeling but Mouse understood what he was trying to do.

"It's just a rumble, it'll stop in a minute but please do a quick head count to make sure everyone is here."

As soon as Arowan had finished speaking, the volcano went back to sleep and everything went eerily silent.

Relief quickly spread across the faces of the people followed by a sudden burst of energy and cheering.

"Angel, what on earth was *that* all about?" Asked Mouse.

"That Mouse," said Arowan as he joined them, "was Volmère's way of reminding us that this is still a volcanic island."

"But it's ok now?"

"Yes." Reassured Arowan.

"We get the odd rumble every so often, not quite as bad as that one though." Said Angel.

"And everyone will just clear away the loose stones that fell and by night time, you'll never know anything happened." Finished Arowan.

Bangus and Trahira joined their dad, sister and Mouse.

"Come on you two," said Arowan as he put a protective arm around the two younger ones, "let's go tidy up."

And the three of them left Angel and Mouse as they headed back to their dwelling to clear away the dust and stones. The same as every family was doing.

"We had better get back and tidy up your dwelling." Suggested Mouse.

"Ok. Then a day here in Bichir. My dad won't let anyone out of here today."

"Fine by me." Replied Mouse gratefully.

"I have some shells, we can sit in the sunshine, swim a bit and make something for you to take back home with you?"

"I'd love that."

So Angel and Mouse did just that.

Once the dwelling was rubble free, they spent the morning swimming with the others and lazing about in the lagoon.

Mouse got to know Angel's friends a little more and they all wanted to know more about Mouse and her world.

Mouse smiled to herself as she thought about Taya reacting the same way when she mentioned her mobile phone. Surprised and confused faces all asking questions about cars, mobiles and shopping.

It was a nice relaxing way to spend a morning after the last few days' adventures.

Just before lunchtime, Angel held out her hand to Mouse.

"Here you are Mouse." She said.

"What is it?"

"Hold your hand out and see."

Mouse held out her hand and Angel dropped a small bracelet into it.

"Oh Angel, it's really pretty!" Exclaimed Mouse as she examined the leathery twine bracelet which had been threaded through three creamy pink shells.

"I thought you might like to keep it as a memento for when you get home?"

"Thankyou," sighed Mouse, "if I ever get home."

*

Inanya felt the underwater cave, her home, tremble and the water quiver. She knew there was trouble ahead. She also knew that it wasn't just the volcano causing tremors of uncertainty throughout the land and sea, which brought a smile to her grey face.

The unfortunate incidents of the previous day had brought her fury to the surface once again and she knew that killing the beautiful young mermaid had been a mistake. She had avoided the shimmery creatures for ages, knowing that their colourful, graceful bodies would just fuel her anger at being stuck in the dark depths of the ocean, and being stuck in a slimy ugly body. She had let her temper overtake her actions and she was determined not to let it happen again. Inanya was clever enough to know that she would never get the girl to retrieve The Trident for her, and set her free at last, if she continued to fight with her land loving friends, and the mer-people.

She would need a different approach.

She needed her 'insider' to help formulate a plan.

*

Bichir had almost returned to normal; some sat on the beach chatting, some were in the water and some were in their dwellings going about their normal daily routines.

But there was a sombre undertone in all they said and did.

As Angel tied the bracelet around Mouse's wrist there was an ear splitting BOOM and the whole lagoon shook for the second time that day!

The only difference being that this was far worse than the last time.

Within seconds the people of Bichir fled from their dwellings, rushed out of the water and all congregated on the beach area, counting heads as they did so.

Angel and Mouse found Arowan, Bangus and Trahira and they huddled close together.

"Dad?" Asked Angel.

"This hasn't happened for years!" He shouted back over the noise of the tremor.

"What do we do?"

"We all need to get through the waterfall and stay in the

water. It's not safe to be in here."

Arowan started ushering people into the water.

"Go through the fall!" He shouted.

The noise was unbearable; a loud rumbling sound which echoed and crashed it's way around the lagoon.

It wasn't long before word spread and the entire population of Bichir was headed into the water. As Mouse looked around the beautiful lagoon she was horrified to see small rocks falling, cracks appearing in the cave walls and streamers of vegetation snaking their way down to the trembling ground.

"Go, go, go!" Shouted Arowan, and he gently pushed his children and Mouse into the water.

"Are you coming dad?"

"Of course Angel, look after Mouse and your brother and sister. I'll just make sure everyone is out."

"Hurry then dad."

Angel, Mouse, Bangus and Trahira waded into the rippling water as the crashes got louder and the ripples in the water turned into small waves, sloshing against the shore. As they swam towards the waterfall they glanced back occasionally to see Arowan darting about, dodging flying rocks, waving away swirling dust and making sure everyone was safe.

As Angel and Mouse reached the waterfall they looked back at Bichir. It was hard to see through the mist of sand and falling debris but they could just make out the shape of Arowan, running and diving into the water at last.

Forgetting her earlier fear of the waterfall's force, Mouse followed everyone else and ducked through the unforgiving water and out the other side to where she had first met Angel. They joined the other frightened villagers, some of whom had plonked youngsters on the shingle areas, whilst the rest of them remained in the pool.

As Arowan emerged through the fall they all heard an almighty CRASH as a rock, somewhere inside Bichir, had fallen from a great height and hit the ground with a ferocious force!

There were a few screams from the youngsters and worried faces all around.

Arowan reached Angel, Mouse, Bangus and Trahira.

"Is everyone ok?" He asked, plopping kisses on the top of all their heads, including Mouse.

They all nodded.

"What are we going to do dad?" Asked Angel.

"After hearing that last rock falling, I think the best thing we can do is head to the beach for now. I have no idea how long this is going to last. We can always swim up river to the fresh water if need be."

Arowan tried to sound convincing but truthfully he was as unsure as the rest of them as to what to do next.

BOOM!

All eyes turned towards the summit of the volcano which could just be seen in the distance above Bichir. The three points of Volmère were smoking but as the villagers watched, a trickle of fiery orange lava spilled from the middle, highest peak.

BOOM!

Splatters of lava erupted like a party popper into the air and scattered around the side of the volcano slopes.

"Dad!" Shrieked Angel.

"It's ok, the lava won't reach this side of the island, the crater slopes lower on the other side so it will naturally run down the other side of the volcano."

Mouse and Angel clung together, not noticing that Tang was watching their every move.

"Let's all get to the beach!" Yelled Arowan.

The people of Bichir obeyed and all of them started to head out of the lagoon.

"Angel," whispered Mouse, "What about the beast things?"

Angel saw the fear on Mouse's face.

"Dad, what about the Verzillas?"

Arowan knew that the herd would move down to the lower grounds for safety but he couldn't and wouldn't say it out loud and end up petrifying everyone even more.

"If we stick together in groups, we'll be ok. They wouldn't take on all of us together."

Angel and Mouse didn't look convinced.

"Come on, let's go. We need to keep together."

They had all been swimming slowly to the edge of the pool, and waiting in family bunches to get out.

Finally the last family were out of the water and waiting for further instruction from Arowan.

"Stay together as best you can, keep alert and head to the beach." He shouted over the still trembling, groaning island.

Mouse took one last glance at the volcano before disappearing into the jungle. The once clear blue sky was now a dusty, smoky grey with the occasional spurt of burning lava, shooting up into the air like a firework.

*

Inanya knew that the people of Bichir, and that meant the girl also, would evacuate and wait out the duration of the eruption at the beach.

She needed to get to Tang.

Knowing their plans would be advantageous when plotting her next move.

She sent some of her serpents up the river, not too far, where the water was still murky enough not to let too much sunlight onto their delicate skin. They were to wait, watch and report back. She also hoped that Tang would come looking for her and she could find out what was going on.

Patience – something she had never been very good at.

*

The grown ups had encouraged the youngsters to go and play in the sea, trying to distract them from the uncertainty of the situation. They didn't need them to be scared and worried too, but they made sure they stayed in the shallows where they could be seen.

Bonito, Vimba and Mora found Angel and Mouse.

"Has anyone seen Tang?" Asked Vimba.

"No – I haven't seen much of him this last few days – he's been really weird." Replied Bonito.

"What's weird is that he's normally stuck to you like glue Angel, and lately we can never find him!" Said Mora who looked at Vimba and winked. They giggled together.

"What are you two laughing at?" Quizzed Angel.

"Oh come on Angel," Vimba looked once again at Mora, "you can't tell me you haven't noticed how he looks at you. How he's always wherever you are?"

"No. No I haven't noticed," defended Angel, "and if that was the case, where is he now, when I would need him the most?" She huffed.

Mouse just listened to the conversation, amused.

"That's why we're asking *you*! He's normally with you and so when we couldn't see him with his family, we automatically look for you." Bonito explained.

"Well, where is he then." It was a statement rather than a question.

"I'm sure he'll show up sooner or later," said Mora, "shall we go for a quick swim, he might be in the water already."

The friends all agreed to go for a dip in the sea and on the request of Arowan, keep a close eye on the younger ones.

Thankfully, without any Oxystemla, no one could go very far.

*

Grateful that after the first volcano shudder of the morning, he had gathered some Oxystemla, Tang had managed to slip away unnoticed. This was only the second time that he had visited the Serpent Queen and he was still very much afraid of her.

Still, he thought, as he swam deeper into the darkest and coldest water, if Angel was too wrapped up in her new friend to notice him, he would have to make sure he did something about it. He approached Inanya's cave and was immediately confronted by two menacing looking serpents. Tang would never get used to how loathsome the black, orange and white creatures were, who protected Inanya, their Queen.

A voice from the depths of the cave got closer as Inanya appeared. Tang would not enter the cave as it was too dark for him to see anything, and he wasn't completely stupid.

"Tang," Inanya hissed through clenched teeth, "what is going on up there?"

Tang explained about the volcano and that Angel and Mouse were in the water with the youngsters.

"They are no good to me without that magical little plant inside them." She spat, "I also need them to trust me."

Tang automatically laughed.

"Silence!" She screeched, and her tail whipped at Tang with some speed which he only just managed to dodge.

"I'm - I'm sorry. It's just that is impossible, especially after what happened yesterday." He stammered.

"That's where you come in my dear. You will help me hatch a plan where I will become their ally," a toothy grin spread across her face, "and as soon as this wretched volcano goes back to sleep, the better."

Tang thought for a moment.

"I think I have the perfect plan..."

They huddled together for a moment, whispering and plotting.

"I must go, or they will worry." Announced Tang.

"Yes dear boy, go back to them and act normally. Let me know as soon as you can when we can put our plan into action."

"Ok." And with that Tang swam away from the serpent queen as fast as he could.

*

Arowan couldn't see the peaks of the volcano from the beach, there were far too many tall trees in the way. But what he did know was that the volcano was quietening down. It was the worse episode that he could ever remember and it would be the same for most of the residents of Bichir. It had been several hours since the first rumble in the early hours and about three hours since they all evacuated.

Everyone had been dipping in and out of the sea but all the salt water was going to dry their skin out soon so they needed to get back to the fresh water as soon as possible.

The silence was notable but disbelieving.

Mouse and Angel had ushered everyone out of the sea and back to their families. Everyone sat in silence, not daring to hope that it was over.

One by one, scattered in groups along the powdery white sand, families turned to Arowan.

"Dad," whispered Angel, "do you think it's safe to return home?"

Arowan looked at all the expectant faces around him, knowing that one wrong decision could prove disastrous.

He lifted his head back and took a deep breath, the air no longer smelt of smoke and he looked up to the sky above the volcano summit, it had already begun to clear.

"I think we should make our way back to the lagoon and make a decision there." And with that, he beckoned to everyone to follow him and his family.

So, with some trepidation the residents of Bichir made their way slowly back to the outer pool.

The jungle was eerily quiet and still, except for the villagers trundling through the large trees and many plants which made up the area around the lagoon.

Once again Mouse found herself marvelling at some of the flowers; their vivid colours, their size and their questionable ability to grow in such a dense environment.

Arowan stood in front of the large group and looked at the

water which was as calm as ever except for the few feet of white bubbling water around the waterfall. He looked once again at the pool, once again at the faces who depended on him and then dove into the cool dark water.

He was followed, almost immediately, by the rest of the crowd who's oooh's and ahhh's signalled the relief of washing away the crusty salt water from their parched skin and delicate fins.

Arowan faced the waterfall.

He was afraid to see what was left of Bichir. Afraid for all his friends.

They all watched as his white blonde head disappeared under the fall.

They all waited in silent anticipation. The whole of the outer lagoon was awash with white bobbing heads like a scattering of pearls from a broken necklace. All eyes focused on the gushing water of the fall.

Suddenly Arowan emerged with a smile on his face.

"It's ok! There are a few rocks where there shouldn't be rocks, and some are quite large, and the tunnel looks as if it could be blocked but it's not too bad, all things considered."

Relief spread, tense shoulders relaxed and worried expressions faded.

So slowly the people returned home to a slightly battered but mostly unscathed Bichir. Mouse watched as the villagers ducked into the waterfall, grateful that these lovely people returned to their home unharmed.

There was no wooping or cheering, just a thankful silence as they moved.

A brief movement caught Mouse's eye – one of the shrubs on the edge of the lagoon rustled and shook.

"Angel," she whispered, "there's something over there." She pointed to the shaking shrub, but before Angel could reply the shrub let out a throaty growl!

Terrified and reminded of the last encounter on the edge of the lagoon, Mouse grabbed onto Angel.

"It's ok Mouse," she said, "if it were a Verzilla it would be making more noise than that."

"What shall we do?"

"Let's just join my dad and help clear up Bichir."

"But what if it's hurt – whatever it is?"

Angel took a moment to consider this possibility.

"Ok," she said, "let's go take a look."

They swam, as quietly as they could, to the edge of the lagoon a little way away from the shrub to see if they could see anything without getting too close.

Angel lifted herself a little way out of the water to get a closer look.

"Oh!" She exclaimed.

"What *is* it?"

"It's a Verzilla."

"Well let's get out of here!" Mouse tried to pull Angel away.

"But it's hurt Mouse."

"I'm not sure if I care if it's head has come off! One of those things tried to eat me not so long ago!"

"I know Mouse, but this one looks in a bad way?" Angel gazed at Mouse with huge sad eyes.

"But what can we actually do Angel?"

"I don't think it can move, and there's blood." And with that Angel freed herself from Mouse's grip and hoisted herself up onto the bank a few feet away from the Verzilla.

"Angel!" Hissed Mouse.

"It's ok, look come and see."

Mouse wasn't entirely sure about this weird situation but she couldn't leave Angel here on her own with this creature whether it was poorly or not.

"Wait for me then." She sighed.

Ungracefully, she heaved herself onto the bank to join Angel.

They both inched closer as quietly as they could. The Verzilla was injured and had a nasty gash on the top of one of his monstrously huge legs. It's breathing was laboured and it's beady eyes were wary as it watched Mouse and Angel getting closer and closer.

"Can we really do anything to help it Angel?"

"I'm not sure."

The beast started to thrash about, sending Angel and Mouse staggering backwards and hurling themselves back into the water!

Shaken up, they swam into the middle of the pool and nearly jumped out of their skins when Arowan shouted from the waterfall "Angel, Mouse, what are you doing? I've been looking for you."

Never more grateful to see her dad, Angel swam to him and clung to him whilst explaining what they'd found.

"Why on earth did you go near it?"

"It's hurt dad."

Arowan looked at Mouse, who shrugged her shoulders and smiled at him. She didn't know what else to do, she could see he was a bit annoyed at their recklessness.

He sighed, "Where is it?"

"Just over there on the bank, I don't think it can get up." Angel said as she pointed to the spot they had just leapt from, only moments before.

"Show me."

Arowan followed the two girls up onto the bank and slowly edged his way towards the injured beast, who had remained quiet and still for the last few minutes.

He saw the cut and the blood flowing from it's leg.

"It looks quite bad girls but I have only ever heard stories of how to get near to these creatures without getting hurt yourself."

"And what were the stories dad?"

"It involves Oxystemla and some of the leaves from the lagoon which we use for bedding and clothes."

"Well, let's go and get some."

"What do we need to do with the Oxystemla Arowan?" Asked Mouse.

"We need to get it to eat it." The girls looked puzzled, Arowan continued, "They have extremely small brains and the amount of oxygen from the plant puts them into a kind of trance as it rushes through it's body. We then cover the wound in the lagoon plants and it seals the wound."

"And does it work?" Asked Mouse.

"I have no idea, it's an old legend from when our ancestors tried to tame them when they were searching for the lost Trident."

"None of them are tame so I presume it didn't work." Said Angel.

"I'm not sure." Said Arowan, "The reason they didn't find The Trident is because they were away from the water for too long. Many have died trying to get their hands on The Trident but not because of the Verzillas."

"Oh." Said Angel and Mouse at the same time.

"So....we can try, if it'll make you two feel better?" Suggested Arowan.

"Well we can't leave it here." Said Angel.

"Ok. Angel, you go back and get some Oxystemla and lagoon plant and Mouse and I will wait here with ... it." Suggested Arowan.

Mouse watched Angel dive into the water, her long legs disappearing into the water gracefully.

"I can't leave you two alone for five minutes can I?" Chuckled Arowan.

"I guess not." Smiled Mouse.

The Verzilla tried to move again by thrashing itself against the ground but it was weaker this time and not as frantic. It let out another long, pained growl.

Angel was back incredibly quickly with the Oxystemla in her pouch and a handful of the plant.

"We need to get this done as soon as possible before this thing lets out another noise and attracts the rest of the herd." Said Arowan.

"How exactly are we going to get it to eat the Oxystemla dad?"

"We need to get some berries and squeeze them over it so it's smells and tastes like something it's used to."

Angel hurried off to the surrounding bushes to find some fruits. She picked some small orange berries, got out the Oxystemla and squeezed the juice of the berries over it.

"Here, give it to me. You two stay here." Said Arowan.

Mouse and Angel stayed where they were and watched Arowan move slowly closer to the now snarling beast. When he was in throwing distance, he launched a scrunched up ball of flavoured Oxystemla and it landed within a foot of the enormous scaly head.

To scared to cheer, Mouse and Angel were just glad when Arowan got back to where they were stood.

The three of them waited for what seemed like an age but eventually the Verzilla caught a whiff of the berry aroma, turned his head and gobbled up the plant in one mouthful.

"How do we know if it's worked dad?" Whispered Angel.

"Watch it's eyes."

They all stood and watched. Angel and Mouse didn't know what they were looking for. But as the beast's eyes stopped darting about they knew they'd seen it. It's eyes were almost glazed over and just staring at the sky.

"I think that must be it." Announced Arowan, "I'll go and wrap the wound in the plant and we'll see what happens."

Arowan still moved carefully and warily towards the Verzilla, just in case, but the beast didn't move a muscle. He bent down and placed the plant on the scaly wound and pressed down gently. He held his hand there for a minute or two before removing his hand and the plant. Remarkably the gash had stopped bleeding and already crusted over in a scab. Arowan, not knowing how long the trance would last for, moved away and back to the girls.

The three of them sat down behind a bush and waited once again.

It all happened so fast.

The Verzilla, all of a sudden, snapped out of its trance and got to its feet. It looked a bit disorientated for a second, stared right at Mouse through the flimsy leaves of the bush, and lumbered back into the jungle.

***

Chapter Six

Bewildered, Arowan, Angel and Mouse stood up from behind the bush not quite trusting what had just happened.

"I wouldn't have believed that if someone had told me the story of the last half an hour." Muttered Arowan.

"Me either." Agreed Angel.

Mouse just said nothing; she hadn't quite recovered from the steely stare the Verzilla gave her before it disappeared from view.

"Come on you two," said Arowan as he put his arms around the girls, "let's get back to Bichir, there's lots to be done."

The three of them made their way to the pool and lowered themselves into the water. They swam to the waterfall and all three ducked through it, into Bichir.

When Angel and Mouse resurfaced on the other side they were shocked to see the devastation of Bichir.

"It's not as bad as it first looks," reassured Arowan as he noticed the looks of horror on both their faces, "it's still structurally ok but needs some repairs here and there."

They swam to the beach together with wide disbelieving eyes as they took in the once hanging streamers of vegetation now floating in the dust covered water, the cracks around the cave walls and the massive amount of debris scattered over the whole of Bichir.

They waded through the shallows and onto the beach where most of the youngsters were huddled together whilst the older ones were making a start on the tidy up.

This wasn't going to be quick and it wasn't going to be easy.

Everyone watched as Arowan walked up the beach area, and noticed his resigned expression change slowly to a determined glare.

"Ok everyone!" He bellowed, "I think the best way to tackle this is for all the women to start on the dwellings and the rest of us make a start on the surrounding areas."

There was some bustling about as everyone went off in different directions and soon enough there was more space on the beach to move about and get on with the clear up.

"I'll go and take a look at the tunnel, " said Arowan, "see what damage has been done." And he headed off towards the tunnel with a few other men trailing behind him.

"Angel," said Mouse, "isn't it dangerous to be climbing the cave walls and going into tunnels so soon after the eruption?"

"I know what you mean," replied Angel, "but my dad wouldn't dream of suggesting anything if he wasn't sure it was safe. These cave walls have been here for hundreds of years, a few cracks won't hurt."

Mouse considered her answer and concluded that she was right, Arowan was a trustworthy leader.

"What shall we do then?" She asked.

"We'll start in my dwelling and then help everyone else."

Mouse and Angel discovered the same as the rest of the women of Bichir. A few smallish boulders had shuddered their way around the floor, some of the shell decorations, once on the cave walls, were now laying on the floor and everything seemed to be covered in a flimsy blanket of dust.

"It's not too bad I suppose." Said Angel.

"It could have been a lot worse. I doubt we'll be able to move these rocks so I hope you like their new positions?" Mouse replied with a giggle.

Angel took a moment to sweep her eyes around her dwelling, smiled and replied, "I would have put them there to begin with if I'd been able to move them myself."

They laughed together and started to pick up the broken shells and small rocks which were dotted about on the floor.

Once all the debris was cleared away they both left the dwelling in search of some inspiration on how to clear away the dusty layer.

A few of the older women were sat on the beach area keeping an eye on the youngsters who were blissfully unaware of the situation and were playing on the beach and in the water. The women were hastily weaving braches together so they roughly resembled broomsticks, and handing them out to everyone to use to try to sweep away some of the smaller debris, they were crude but they were better than nothing at all.

Bichir was like an ant's nest; trails of people passing rogue rocks along lines, others scurrying about – to and fro, and a few were scaling the rock faces to get to their little homey nooks.

Angel and Mouse did the best they could with the makeshift broom and soon the dwelling was looking almost back to normal. They headed off back to the beach to see if they could help anyone else.

They could hear Arowan's voice from inside the tunnel, which, if the stones and rocks coming out of there was anything to go by, meant the tunnel had been blocked quite badly.

Angel and Mouse joined the long line coming out of the tunnel and helped pass the rocks, which at the end of the line, got unceremoniously plopped into the lagoon. The same lagoon that was filled with the youngsters of Bichir, who apart from dodging the hurled rocks, were armed with spongy like balls which they were sweeping across the surface of the water. The balls seemed to soak up and gather the film of dust which lay on top, which left streaks of crystal clear water amongst the remaining murky surface.

Finally Arowan and five other men appeared from the tunnel, dusty and dirty, and desperately needing to get in the water to hydrate their skin and their fins.

"Is it clear dad?" Asked Angel.

"Clear enough to get through but now it's a bit more of a tighter squeeze for us bigger ones!" He grinned and then took a running jump and dove head first into the refreshing water with a huge splash. He was quickly followed by the other five dusty men.

While the work on the tunnel paused for a while Angel took the opportunity to take a swim herself. She spotted

Tang, who had been watching her and Mouse from the pool. She swam over to him and gave him a playful splash in the face.

"Don't Angel!" He snarled at her. He wasn't sure he could cope with her being all friendly with him just because Mouse wasn't around.

"What on earth is the matter Tang? Are you ok?" She asked, a little hurt.

"Leave me alone," he scowled, "go back to your *other* friend." He swam off, leaving Angel confused and alone.

The next thing she knew she was being dive bombed from above as Bonito, Vimba and Mora sploshed into the water with loud shrieks.

"What's up Angel?" Asked Vimba as soon as she surfaced, wiped her long white hair from out of her eyes and noticed Angels' face.

"I have no idea. I swam over to Tang, who then shouted at me and then left!" She replied.

"That's weird," said Bonito, "I wonder what his problem is lately!"

"He's probably just a bit jealous of you spending time with Mouse, that's all, his nose has been pushed out of joint." Suggested Mora.

Little did she know how true that statement was, but on a much deeper level.

At that moment they were joined by Mouse who could sense something wasn't quite right immediately.

"Why is everyone looking so serious?" She asked. Her four new friends didn't want to worry her so they blamed their frowns on the day's events and troubles, which Mouse accepted.

The five of them splashed around in the water for a while

and terrorised some of the youngsters playfully until they all realised how late it must be; they suddenly noticed long shadows being cast across the cave walls as the sunlight from above dimmed. They all made their way to the beach.

It had been a very eventful day and a very long day, and no one was more grateful than Mouse when she saw Arowan emerge from the tunnel, for the second time that day, with a long stick across his back which was weighed down fish which had obviously been previously cooked and stored.

"Here we go," he said as he plonked the heavy stick down on a rock on the beach, "let's all pitch in and get these wrapped up and on the fire, this is all that's left."

"Come on Mouse, we'll get some vine leaves and I'll show you what to do." Said Angel as she leapt to her feet and grabbed Mouse by the hand. They headed towards the small cave where the Oxystemla grew but passed it and ventured in to the bushes that surrounded it.

"Here," said Angel as she stopped in front of the cave wall a little further on, "these are what we need to pick."

Angel grabbed a leafy, dangly plant which started somewhere way up high and gracefully hung to the ground.

"Just pinch the leaf where it joins the stem and twist and pull." She showed Mouse what she meant. Mouse tried and the leaves came away easily. Before long they had gathered enough vine leaves to wrap the fish in, to cook, and returned to the beach with their stash.

Mouse loved the way everyone merged together; as she watched, there were all ages wrapping fish, the older ones preparing fruits and berries, and the men getting the roaring fire started with a big basket held aloft to place the fish in. As each fish was ready it was passed to one of the women who carefully placed it in the basket above the fire. Mouse marvelled at the harmony in which these lovely villagers existed ... no one would ever believe that only a few hours ago their homes were under threat of being destroyed under a pile of rubble or wiped away by a fatal stream of lava.

The evening, what remained of it, was as enjoyable as the previous evenings. Mouse surprised herself by liking the taste of the vine leaves which, when cooked over the natural fire, were crispy and fishy flavoured. And although the fish wasn't the same as when it was cooked fresh, it was still a surprisingly delicious meal. They all finished off what was left of the stored fish and rounded off the meal with juicy berries. After the food and the subdued conversation everyone went for a swim before going their separate ways to their dwellings. Mouse didn't even care that her stone bed wasn't soft, they'd had an exhausting day, and both she and Angel were fast asleep in no time.

*

Inanya knew that the tunnel to Bichir had been blocked because her serpents had tried to go through it earlier that day, before the villagers had returned, to assess the damage to the lagoon. She also knew that Arowan's priority would be to clear it as soon as he could to allow them to hunt, without having to trek through the treacherous jungle. She couldn't risk sending her serpents to Bichir that night, she assumed that Arowan and the others would be on a high alert for the next 24 hours.

So she stayed put, in her dark cave, hatching a plan. She

would need to meet with Tang for it to work and was hopeful that he would accompany the hunters tomorrow regardless of whether they had to get to the ocean through the jungle or the tunnel.

Inanya was impatient, she was greedy and she was ruthless.

If her plan worked, she would have those idiots from Bichir, and the girl, eating out of her bony, cold hand.

*

The next morning was met with some trepidation by the people of Bichir. It had been less than 24 hours since the first taster of what lay ahead for them. It was almost as if everyone awoke in slow motion, testing each move they made before they made it, searching the surroundings for any sign of disturbance before they proceeded.

After a while, most of the villagers were gathered on the beach for breakfast after their morning dip. It was the quietest meal that Mouse had ever sat through since arriving. Everyone was listening out for unusual sounds and suspicious smells so when there was CRACK from within the tunnel, almost everyone was on their webbed feet in a split second!

It was like clockwork; all the villagers stood up, all the white heads turned to Arowan.

"Ssshh." He whispered, and slowly crept towards the tunnel.

Mouse decided that one of her mum's expressions was meant for this very moment – she really could have heard a pin drop.

Instead of a pin dropping though, Tang bounded through

the opening of the tunnel, waist high in water, holding several fish in his hands.

The sigh of relief was palpable throughout Bichir. Then the wrath of Arowan became apparent.

"Tang, what on earth were you doing?" He shouted, "not only is it dangerous to hunt on your own at the moment, you know never to go to the ocean this early, there are too many unsavoury hunters in the sea at this time of day!"

Unnerved by two things; Arowan shouting at him and being aware that every pair of eyes, bar none, was staring at him, Tang was glad he'd had the foresight to hunt. It had proven to be a great cover, to hide what he had actually been doing.

Angel rushed over to Tang.

"It's ok dad, he's fine and I expect he just went hunting to restock our supplies, right Tang?"

"Um, yes," muttered Tang, annoyed that Angel had jumped in to defend him when he could have handled the situation himself, "I'm sorry Arowan, I just thought I was helping." He hung his head, playing the part splendidly.

"Ok, ok Tang. No harm done this time. Take the fish to the storage area and we'll prepare them later." Replied Arowan.

Relieved, Tang shoved past Angel and glared at Mouse as he went to put the fish away.

Arowan watched him go with a confused look on his face, he had never seen Tang behave badly towards Angel before, he'd always thought that he had a bit of a crush on her. This was strange behaviour but then, he reasoned, it had been a strange few days.

While he had everyone together he forgot about Tang and he addressed his fellow villagers.

"Today I will go and hunt with five other experienced and strong hunters. I suggest everyone else stays close to Bichir. Is that ok?"

All heads nodded except for Angels.

"Can we come too dad, please?" She asked.

"Absolutely not Angel, it's not safe at all."

"But we..."

"This isn't a discussion. Stay here with Mouse and your friends and look after Bangus and Trahira."

The look in his eyes made Angel think twice about arguing so she just nodded her head and slumped back down on the beach next to Mouse.

"Let's go for a swim Angel," said Mouse trying to cheer her up, "we can have races with the others and then play games with Bangus and Trahira?"

Angel looked mildly interested, "I suppose so."

"I think we've had far too much excitement the last few days, I'm ready for a nice relaxing day just messing about in the pool."

"Ok, I suppose I can do that, but that's not going to find you a way to get home is it?"

Angel had struck a nerve.

Mouse's once happy face clouded over.

"I'm so sorry Mouse!" Angel cried, "I didn't mean that, I really didn't!"

"It's ok. I suppose I just get so comfortable whatever world I'm in, that going home is a distant hope, or in this case, an impossibility at the moment. It's not like we're any closer to finding out how to get me home is it?"

"I'm sure there's a way, and I'm sure my dad will come across it very soon Mouse," she pleaded, "we're obviously just not on the right track at the moment."

Mouse looked at Angel, "We're not really on any track Angel. I have no idea how to get home."

Angel wrapped her arms around Mouse and thought how brave she was and how grown up she seemed, but then Mouse had had adventures, and been put in situations, that the rest of them could only imagine.

They were interrupted by the sudden appearance of Bangus and Trahira. Angel let go of Mouse and looked fondly at her brother and sister.

"Dad said we're to stick to you like glue while he's hunting." Said Banguṣ with a self important grin.

Mouse giggled.

"Looks like they're looking after you!" She said to Angel.

"We'll see about that!" Roared Angel as she chased after her younger brother and sister, waving her arms about, delighting in the squeals coming from them as they all ended up diving head first into the lagoon.

*

Arowan and his friends got their weapons and a supply of Oxystemla for their fishing expedition, and set off into the tunnel.

There were still a few sections of the tunnel where the gap had been narrowed slightly but the boulders that had shifted and fallen were too big to move.

They were all glad to get out of the confined space and out into the river which looked remarkably untouched by the volcanic eruption. The clear fresh water still flowed gently to the sea and the vegetation along each side of the riverbank still looked lush and green in the sunshine.

They made their way to the rock, ate some Oxystemla and

103

dove back into the now slightly murkier water. As strong swimmers they swam through the turbulent crashing together of the river meeting the ocean.

Arowan had decided to go into deeper water where the lager fish were plentiful. They needed to restock their supplies after the eruption had rendered most of the stored fish inedible, due to the dust and rocks which had fallen on it.

The men, revelling in the freedom of the open sea, swam fast and strong and before long, reached the spot where Arowan suggested they dive and start fishing. It was not a usual hunting ground for them but once underwater they knew it would be perfect to catch large quantities of bigger fish. The seaweed was tall and billowy and the coral was colourful and dense.

The perfect terrain for fish.

Unlike Angel and her friends, there was no messing about. They were serious hunters, helping each other herd shoals of different species into traps and spearing them mercilessly.

One by one fish were caught and placed into their nets to take back to Bichir. Tonight's feast would be a good one.

Pleased that the trip had been successful and not taken as long as he had anticipated, Arowan signalled to the others that they should head back home.

But as they came together to fasten and secure their nets and test the weight of their bounty, they failed to notice the glint of a blade as it came swiftly from behind one of Arowan's friends and sliced across his chest!

Arowan's friend, Albacore, yowled in pain as the blood instantaneously coloured the surrounding water a deep red.

Arowan and the others rushed towards him, startled.

Within seconds they were all surrounded.

Not by serpents.

Not by mer-people.

But by a mixture of the two. A half breed creature who, some generations ago, had mixed the two species together resulting in a slithery serpent like creature with the odd feature from the mer-people. They were predominantly serpent with the long slippery body but with a mermaids tail and long powerful arms. They had the colourings of the serpents; the flecks of orange and white in their black bodies but their arms were a grey fleshy colour with long spiny fingers. An ugly evil species that everyone avoided at all costs if possible.

Arowan had encountered these creatures only once before many years ago, when he had been hunting with his father. They were bloodthirsty and soulless, and his father had found that out first hand.

Arowan reached for his own knife but was stopped as a grey spiny hand, stronger and more powerful than it looked, came from behind him and clamped over his, stopping him making any further move.

The serpillion held fast and twisted its long body around to face Arowan.

"Oh no you don't!" It hissed.

Arowan quickly moved his head to see past this hideous creature to see what was happening to Albacore. All he could see was all five of them being roughly tied up with long thick vines. He turned to face his captor.

"What do you want?" He hissed back, "We've only come to fish!"

"But this is our fishing territory Arowan. Not yours."

"How do you know who I am?" Asked Arowan, a little surprised at this familiarity.

"Never mind that. We don't allow anyone to fish in these waters, not even you!"

"Keep the fish then, but let us go. We won't ever come back."

"We don't need your fish. We just don't like intruders."

Arowan was very aware of the extreme danger they were in and also realised that their Oxystemla wasn't going to last forever. He could also see the pain in Albacore's eyes as the blood continued to flow freely from his body.

"So what exactly are you going to do with us?" He asked tentatively.

The other serpillions started to gnash their teeth together and began to squirm about in a frenzy. Arowan was rarely scared but right at this moment, he feared for their lives. If these creatures didn't kill them, then being underwater for too much longer would.

"I haven't decided yet but I think this..." He thrust his sharp knife into Arowan's thigh, "...should give you some idea!"

Arowan yelled out in pain as the serpillion yanked the blade straight out again. It was becoming increasingly difficult to see underwater as thick blood mixed with water, which was now pouring from two nasty injuries.

"This is what we do to trespassers Arowan." Spat the serpillion, right up close to Arowan's face.

"Ok. Ok, I get it, and I think you've proven that you don't tolerate anyone in this area of the sea, but please, let us go and we'll never return?" Pleaded Arowan.

"Mmm, an interesting idea," smirked the serpillion, "but I don't know that for sure do I? The best way would be to make sure you never came back by myself. And the only way to do that is to kill you and your air breathing friends."

Arowan tried to struggle free but soon realised it was useless. The creatures spiny hand had still been wrapped around his own but now let go and instructed the others of his kind to strip the captives of their various weaponry. Arowan and his friends were pushed and pulled about, as one by one, their spears and knives fell to the sea bed, way below. They were, once again, held in vice like grips so as not to escape.

"Let's go!" Instructed the leader.

"Where are you taking us?" Shouted Arowan, mindful of the amount of blood in the water and the fact they wouldn't last much longer without some more Oxystemla.

"We have families to feed too you know!" The toothy sneer and the steely glare was pure evil.

The friends were yanked by their bindings and pulled along, helplessly, by the slimy serpillions, towards certain and painful deaths.

Whilst being pulled along in the water together, Arowan was able to get a better look at Albacore. He didn't look good at all, his body was limp and he was losing far too much blood. The gash across his chest had opened up and showed just how deep the knife had struck.

Arowan was desperately trying to think of a way out of this because if they continued to flavour the sea with blood they would be dealing with far greater predators than these serpillions. The memories came flooding back from a few days ago when the enormous shark had picked up the scent of the small amount of blood that day. Why they hadn't been surrounded by the horrific creatures by now, was a mystery to him.

Frustrated that he couldn't reach out to help his dear friend, Arowan was about to ask Albacore how he was holding up and to tell him to hang in there, when all of a sudden one of Inanya's serpents shot past them from out of nowhere!

Within seconds more serpents had appeared.

Then Inanya herself.

"Oh brilliant. Just what we need." Muttered Arowan, "Two evil idiots fighting over who gets to kill us first."

Arowan had just about given up hope that they would survive this, but was keen enough to see who would lose this particular fight and pay with their lives, the same as they were going to. He knew these serpillions were monstrous but he had also seen Inanya's deathly fury.

But to his total amazement, Inanya came fast and strong, straight towards his own captor, and crashed into him with full force! The impact jerked him from the vice like grip and catapulted him away from the serpillion.

Still bound by the strong twine he could only watch as Inanya's serpents set upon the serpillions. There were approximately three serpents to every serpillion, and it wasn't long before every serpillion had at least one serpent's pointy sharp teeth sunk deep into its body! Arowan watched as both types of eel like creatures writhed in battle, twisting and jolting together until one by one, broken and half devoured bodies drifted downwards, lifelessly.

Other serpents had been busy biting through the knotted twine which had held them captive and soon all of Arowan's friends had been freed.

Finally Arowan's hands were also free and he dished out a

portion of Oxystemla immediately to all his friends. It was not ideal to eat it under the water and certainly not in sea water but they could not afford to be picky. He was about to flee the scene and get Albacore's wound tended to as soon as possible, when his attention was drawn to Inanya, who was wrestling with the leader of the serpillions.

He couldn't quite believe what he was witnessing but he could just make out that Inanya had been bitten several times along the length of her slippery, spiny tail but she was not yet defeated. But it was becoming increasingly difficult to see what was actually going on due to the sea turning crimson. He was torn between getting Albacore home and seeing who would be the victor in this violent battle. He was confused about why Inanya had come to their rescue and stubborn curiosity was keeping him rooted to the spot.

Then he saw it.

The serpillion didn't.

Inanya managed to bring her long spear from behind her and push it through the water with great strength. The spear hit its intended target and more dark red blood blocked his view.

Mouths' agape, the six friends could only watch as Inanya emerged through the swirling red water, like headlights through a thick fog. Arowan and his friends had no weapons so they all instinctively moved together to form a protective shield around Albacore.

"Arowan." Said Inanya.

"I don't know *what* is going on here or what you could possibly want Inanya, but we are unarmed, injured and seriously not in the mood for another confrontation."

"Arowan, I'm not going to fight you. I saw that you were

109

in trouble and I ..."

"You what Inanya?"

"...I wanted to make up for the other day. You know - the mer-maid."

Unable to comprehend this bizarre situation, Arowan didn't know what to say. He looked at his friends. They looked as bewildered as he was.

"Well if you're not going to cause any trouble for us, then we need to be heading back to Bichir."

"Of course Arowan. Let us help you."

"No!" Arowan held up his hand to halt her as she made a move to come closer to them, "Thankyou but we're fine."

"Ok, as you wish."

Puzzled Arowan couldn't help but ask again, "Why Inanya? Why after all this time, and after..." He gulped, "after Tilapia?"

"Like I said, I'm tired of being enemies, I just wanted to make up for all the things I've done."

She hung her head in false shame, her jet black hair hiding the true expression on her face. Her serpents were silently applauding her performance.

"Nothing will ever make up for depriving Angel of her mother, but, I do thank you for today and for certainly saving our lives."

Inanya nodded, "I understand."

"It will take time to mend the bridges we have built between our different kinds over the centuries, but after today I am prepared to at least try to get along if you are?"

"I'll do anything, as I think you'll agree, I have shown you today." She flicked her blood drenched tail towards him as visual proof of her act of kindness.

Arowan softened and nodded his head towards her as a

gesture of goodwill.

"It seems we both need to tend to our injuries, so if you don't mind, I need to get back."

"I agree." Satisfied that today had been a resounding success, Inanya turned away from Arowan before an evil grin crept across her face.

Arowan and his friends watched her and her serpents swim off into the distance. Convinced they were far enough away and without waiting another moment they swam back to where they had been relieved of their weapons and their catch and hastily gathered everything back together.

And with blood still flowing freely from Arowan and Albacore, and realising the still very serious danger they were in, the six men swam as fast as they were able back to the shore, back up the river and then made their way through the tunnel.

*

As the six men emerged it didn't take long before they were surrounded by extremely concerned villagers.

"Get help for Albacore, his wound is deep and he's been bleeding for a while now. He has lost a lot of blood." Yelled Arowan above the noise, "And would someone take the catch from us and get it ready for later."

Questions were coming from all directions but Arowan was tired and wounded himself. He just about summoned up the strength to hug Angel with all his might as she pushed through the crowd and flung herself at him.

"Dad." She sighed.

"I'm ok. I'm ok." He said, "Where are my other two

misfits?"

"They're with Mora. When we saw you come through the tunnel, and saw the blood, we decided to distract them until you get cleaned up."

"Good girl." He said proudly.

"What on earth happened dad?"

"Let's get this wound cleaned, make sure Albacore is ok and then we'll gather on the beach and tell everyone together. It's a story they'll all want to hear."

"Ok, come on then, let me help you sort out your leg."

Before they shuffled off to Arowan's dwelling, they made sure that Albacore had been helped away by his family. He would be weak for some time but would rest completely and be looked after until such time as he had recovered.

As Angel washed Arowan's thigh, as gently as she could, she couldn't help asking Arowan what had happened.

"If it hadn't happened to me, I would never have believed it." And that was all he would say.

Knowing not to push her dad, Angel was satisfied that the wound was clean and she wrapped it in the same lagoon plant they had used on the Verzilla not so long ago.

She helped him to his feet and they went back out to the beach together where they found Mouse frantically searching for them.

"I wondered where you had gone, are you ok Arowan?" She asked, worried.

"I'm fine Mouse. But I am starving so let's get these fish cooking." He smiled at her warmly. He rallied all the villagers together, who were eagerly waiting to hear what had happened, and within minutes everyone was preparing for their meal and a story. There were vine leaves, fish and fruits and the smell made his stomach

112

growl but he needed to find Bangus and Trahira, who were still blissfully unaware of the day's events.

Arowan made his way to Mora's dwelling and as he peered quietly into the cave, he saw two young faces captivated by Mora's story. It reminded him of when their mum used to story-tell when they were smaller.

Arowan felt a gentle tug on his heart strings.

Both Bangus and Trahira were sat cross legged on the floor of the dwelling with wide eyes and mouths open. Arowan decided that whatever Mora's story was about, it was obviously a good one – Bangus and Trahira were rarely as quiet as this !

"Knock knock!" He announced.

"Dad!" Bangus and Trahira leapt to their feet and ran to Arowan and wrapped him in a hug.

"Thankyou Mora." He mouthed over their heads, Mora smiled and nodded back.

As Trahira stepped back from Arowan she said "Dad, Mora was telling us this amazing story where..." She stopped mid sentence as she glanced down at Arowan's thigh, "What happened to your leg?"

"Ah, just a little scratch that looks worse than it is, it doesn't hurt."

"How did you do it?" Asked Bangus.

"Well, we've had a bit of an adventure today."

"Another one?" Bangus looked worried.

"Well, yes, another one," Arowan ruffled his 10 year olds white hair, "now come to the beach and I'll tell you all about it."

"Another story?" Trahira couldn't believe her luck, two stories in one day, but too young to really understand the implications of what had happened to Arowan and his friends that day.

"Yes another story, now come on you two."

Arowan took Bangus and Trahira by the hands and Mora followed behind.

By the time they got back to the beach, fish were being cooked over the fire, bowls of berries and fruits were ready and everyone looked a little bit nervous.

The normally relaxed atmosphere had been replaced by an anxious, jittery feeling.

Arowan was very proud of his fellow villagers because the last few days had been anything but normal for them. The arrival of Mouse had affected everything, even, it seemed, the island itself. Arowan wondered why she had been sent here, he wondered about the effect she'd had on their lives, and most importantly, how he was going to get her back to her world.

As everyone sat down with bowls of steaming fish, all eyes were on him and the silence engulfed him.

"Ok. I'll tell you what happened today, but you're going to find it very hard to believe."

No one said a word.

Arowan recounted the events of the day and there were murmurs of bewilderment and shock throughout the telling of the story.

As he finished, he looked around at all his friends and just said, "Unbelievable really."

"What's unbelievable, " said one villager, "is that there were no sharks attracted to all that blood in the water!"

An entire blanket of white heads nodded in agreement and muttered their astonishment.

"It must be the tide and the flow of the current, if the sharks weren't near the island and the current was pulling strongly in the opposite direction to them, then maybe that had something to do with it?" Suggested another villager.

"Perhaps." Agreed Arowan.

"Whatever the reason, you were extremely lucky."

"I know," Said Arowan, "but regardless of the lack of sharks, Albacore wasn't so lucky."

"He's resting and the blood has dried, so he'll be ok, in time Arowan," said Albacore's brother, "he's being well looked after."

"Tell him, when you see him, that we all wish him well, and not to worry." All the villagers agreed and there were offers of help for the family from everyone.

"Thankyou," said his brother, "I'll tell him."

"I just don't understand why Inanya would be so nice." Said a little voice.

All eyes swivelled from Arowan to Mouse.

"It's certainly a mystery to me." Replied Arowan.

"She was so cruel the other day, what happened, what changed her?"

"I'm not sure Mouse, but she said she was tired of all the fighting between us and I, for once, agree with her."

"It does seem odd though dad." Said Angel.

"That's not the only thing that's odd." Mumbled Arowan.

"What do you mean?"

"Well, Inanya, just showing up like that. Right on cue?"

Again the sea of white heads bobbed up and down together.

"I mean, that's definitely not one of her usual haunts."

A group discussion followed, questioning most of the events of the day.

Something just didn't 'fit'.

Only one person didn't need to ask any questions.

Only one person knew exactly how Inanya had known where to go to lay in wait, for the perfect opportunity.

And only one person hoped that all this risk would pay off and *that* girl would go back to her own world and leave them well alone once again.

*

Inanya's slashes to her tail had been covered and protected by seaweed. Her loyal serpents had seen to her immediately, as soon as they had arrived back to the cave. The serpents were always fearful of Inanya, she was an unpredictable Queen with evil coursing through her veins, but she was positively jubilant in spite of her injuries. They enjoyed her mood but remained wary.

"Tomorrow," she announced, "we will ask to meet with Arowan and the girl."

"What about Tang?" Asked the largest serpent.

"I have no use for him now and he's served his purpose, he got me closer to Arowan but he must vanish now."

"Yes Queen."

"Wait until after I have met with the girl though, then get rid of him. I don't care how you do it!"

"Of course."

"There must be no trace."

"That goes without saying."

An eerie smile crept slowly across Inanya's face.

"We'll soon be free of this wretched curse and be able to bask in the sunlight for the first time."

***

Chapter Seven

After the rollercoaster that had been the last few days, a quiet day in Bichir was planned. The early morning sun shone through the gaping hole in Bichir's ceiling and signalled that a new day had arrived.

There were still a few reminders of the eruption a few days ago but the lagoon's water still glistened, the remaining hanging vegetation gently swayed around the walls, and already the familiar plop of someone taking a dip, could be heard.

As Mouse left Angel's dwelling she looked back at Angel, still fast asleep, and left the dangling leaves across the entrance.

She wandered slowly down to the beach area and saw that preparations for breakfast were well underway.

"Morning Mouse," said Arowan as he appeared from his dwelling, "did you sleep ok?"

"Yes thankyou."

"Is Angel not with you?" He looked about, getting used to the fact there where there was Mouse, there was usually Angel.

"She's still asleep, so I've left her alone while I take a swim."

"Good idea, breakfast won't be long," he smiled, "the smell of that usually wakes her!"

They laughed together easily and then went their separate ways.

Mouse waded into the shallow water, delighting in the cool freshness of the water which was in complete contrast to the heat of the sun which was now beating down on her head.

Soon she was swimming to the middle of the pool. She wasn't alone but there were only a handful of villagers who had also braved an early morning dip so far.

Mouse decided to swim a few circuits of the pool so she made her way to the waterfall and started in a clockwise direction around the edge.

The peace and quiet this time of the day allowed her to take in fully, the beauty of Bichir; it's craggy rock walls which reflected the water from the pool and made the walls dance with light, the array of plant life in all colours either dangling or rooted to the spot, and the shaft of brilliant sunlight which forced its way through the rock and down into the lagoon.

As Mouse swam around the pool she had said a few 'hellos' to passing villagers having a relaxing swim just as she was, but she wasn't ready for the vice like grip and the cold hard stare which confronted her when Tang reached out from nowhere to stop her in her tracks.

"Oh my goodness Tang! You made me jump." She gasped

and smiled.

Tang did not smile back.

"Where's Angel?" He barked.

"She's still asleep ... is there something wrong?"

"Not yet." And with that he let go of her arm and swam off as if nothing had happened.

Bewildered, Mouse decided to go and wake up Angel, to see if she knew what was going on with her strange friend.

By the time she reached the dwelling, Angel was already up and heaving her moist woven leaf blanket off the rocky bed.

"Morning," said Mouse, "what are you doing with that?"

"I'm going to take it to the pool today, it'll need replacing soon but a good soaking in the lagoon water will make it last just that little bit longer."

"Oh ok, do you need some help carrying it to the water?"

"Yes please Mouse."

They both grabbed hold of an end each and dragged it to the pool, arranged it so it wouldn't sink or float away and then wandered to the beach area where breakfast was almost ready to be served. They sat on a large rock by the water while they waited for everyone to gather.

"Angel?"

"Mmmm."

"Tang stopped me while I was swimming earlier and he was a bit weird."

"How do you mean, weird?"

"He grabbed hold of my arm really hard and when I asked him if there was anything wrong, he just stared at me and said – not yet!"

Angel looked puzzled, "I don't know what's the matter with him lately, he's been acting really odd for the last few

119

days."

"I don't think he likes me at all."

"Tang likes everyone Mouse," she stopped what she was saying and thought for a moment, "but he's been grumpy and he has kept his distance from me since you arrived."

"But why?"

"I don't know but I'll ask him later, and try to find out what he meant earlier. Don't worry, I expect my dad would say it's all down to him growing up and the changes boys go through!" She smiled trying to lighten the atmosphere.

"I just don't want you to fall out because of me Angel." Mouse looked saddened.

"Like I said, don't worry. He'll get over it."

Mouse and Angel spent the next few hours sat on the beach with everyone else. They enjoyed a good breakfast and good company and casual visits to the pool. The news on Albacore was positive and Arowan's leg was healing nicely. And even though the last week had been a shock for all of them, the relaxed atmosphere in Bichir was slowly seeping back, the villagers firmly believing that nothing bad could happen anymore, especially after what they'd all endured recently.

Mora, Bonito and Vimba had joined Mouse and Angel and they were all discussing Inanya, the Serpent Queen, and her almost unbelievable change of heart.

"Just seems odd to me," said Bonito, "after all these years of her being the enemy, after doing what she did to your mum Angel, and the same relationship we've had with her ancestors for generations, to suddenly want to be friends *now* is just weird."

Angel looked down at her hands in her lap and twisted her

long webbed fingers together. The pain of remembering what happened to her mother over Inanya's petty jealousy always stung whenever she thought about it but it was a very long time ago now.

"It does seem odd, especially now, with Mouse arriving, the volcano erupting and everything," replied Vimba breaking Angel's train of thought, "but maybe she *is* just tired of all the fighting?" She looked around at her friends who all reluctantly agreed that it was a possibility.

"But that doesn't explain Tang's behaviour lately." Muttered Angel, almost to herself.

"True," said Mora, "Inanya's not the only one acting out of character at the moment."

The friends all nodded.

"Where is he anyway?" Asked Bonito.

"Mouse was the last to see him this morning," said Angel, "tell them what he did and said Mouse."

Mouse told the story of her encounter with Tang a few hours earlier.

"I think we should find him and find out what this is all about once and for all," Suggested Vimba, "he can't go round frightening our visitor for *any* reason, it's so unlike him."

They all agreed and got up from the rocks and went in search of Tang.

*

Arowan was gathering a hunting party together. They needed to restock after the eruption but going out to sea to hunt was not an option, the situation was still too fragile. Arowan had fished up the river before but the salt water

121

fish were much more tasty than the freshwater fish. But he didn't have the luxury of choice, they had to hunt the river fish for now.

So with Bangus and Trahira safely playing with the other youngsters and being kept watch over by the other villagers, Arowan and his friends walked towards the tunnel, knives and spears aplenty.

There was still some major work to be done in the tunnel and once they'd squeezed through, instead of turning left towards the ocean, they all turned right, up river.

There were a different variety of fish in the freshwater of the river, very much edible but not a favourite of the Bichir palate. But food was food and no one was going to risk their lives by going out to sea.

Arowan and his three friends swam against the natural flow of the water which was quite hard going but as they were all strong and relatively healthy, bar a few scrapes and cuts, they made it to 'the bowl'. The bowl was a rounded widening of the river about the size of the lagoon's pool. The strength of the current was still testing in the centre of the bowl shaped area so Arowan and the others swam to one side where the pull was less powerful.

The men hadn't needed to bring any Oxystemla as they would just be diving in short bursts, hopefully spearing a fish, and then resurfacing.

They all tried, unsuccessfully, for about half an hour.

"Where are all the fish Arowan?" One of the men asked.

"I've no idea, unless the recent volcanic activity has got something to do with it," replied a confused Arowan, "let's keep at it for a while longer."

With that four men dove downwards, their large colourful fins emerging above the water for a second, and then they were gone.

They tried another four or five dives each but each time they all came up empty handed.

They swam to the riverbank to catch their breath and decide on plan of action. But as they got closer to the edge it became very clear what had happened to all the fish. For there, stretched along the whole riverbank, were dead fish. All the varieties of fish that they were trying to catch and more species that they'd never even seen before were just lying there, decaying, in the heat of the sun.

The strange thing was that the fishy corpses weren't floating in the water where you'd expect them to be but actually on land as if the fish had literally hurled themselves clean out of the river and onto the grassy/shingly land.

"Whoa!" Exclaimed Arowan, "What on earth happened here?"

"Must have been something to do with the eruption," Suggested another, "what else could it be?"

They all looked puzzled and just couldn't trust their eyes as they continued to scan the view along the riverbank in disbelief.

A low rumbling growl snapped them back to reality with a jolt as they realised they were not alone in hunting the fresh water fish.

The rotting fish flesh was letting off a foul stench which had obviously attracted the herd of Verzillas. So as the bushes close by began to shake and the ground began to shudder, Arowan and his friends took this as the perfect time to leave.

Just as they pushed away from the land, two enormous Verzillas thundered into view, with gnashing jaws and tendrils of drool dangling from their huge mouths, obvious desire for this tasty feast which almost just landed in their laps.

Arowan and his friends watched them from a safe distance as the two Verzillas were joined by another. The first two paid no attention to them but the third watched them as they bobbed about in the water, fighting not to be swept away by the current.

The third Verzilla and Arowan's eyes locked with instant recognition, and as it moved, Arowan noticed the recent injury, now healed, at the top of its leg.

The beast stared for only a moment and then joined in the noisy, ill mannered feasting.

Arowan and his friends finally let themselves drift back down the river towards the tunnel, disappointed with their lack of success but relieved that they weren't amongst the fishy corpses being devoured by three very large, very hungry Verzillas right now!

*

Angel, Mouse, Bonito, Mora and Vimba had searched the whole of Bichir for Tang but he was nowhere to be seen and even his family had not seen him for ages.

They had hunted in all the dwellings, they had ventured a small way into the tunnel and they had swum out to the outer lagoon – but no sign of him anywhere.

They were all sat on the beach when Arowan and his friends emerged, empty handed, through the tunnel.

The villagers who were also sat on the beach with Angel, Mouse and her friends looked at the returning hunters, puzzled.

Never before had Arowan been hunting and come back with nothing!

Arowan felt all eyes upon him. He saw the look in everyone's eyes.

"No fish." He simply stated with long arms and webbed fingers held out to the side of him.

"None at all?" Asked a villager.

"Nope." Replied Arowan, "I think the eruption must have had something to do with it." He then explained what they had found and who else they'd encountered.

Mouse visibly shivered, "I hate those things." She admitted.

"And they ate all of our fish?" Asked Angel.

"They were too rotten for us to eat anyway, so let the Verzillas have them."

"So what are we going to eat dad?"

"Well, there's only one thing we can do and I'm not happy about it, but we're going to have to go and hunt in the ocean."

There were murmurs of concern throughout the gathered villagers.

"It's our only option I'm afraid, but we'll have to make it quick and stay close to our normal hunting waters."

Angel followed her dad while he collected the various different hunting equipment needed for hunting in the sea, longer and much sharper weapons. And she explained that they had 'lost' Tang.

"He's definitely been a bit odd lately." Said Arowan.

"He was weird with Mouse this morning but no one has seen him since."

"He's probably sulking somewhere Angel, he'll come back when he's ready."

"But you said so yourself, it's dangerous to be anywhere on your own at the moment."

"It is, but he's not stupid, he'll be careful."

"Mmmm, what has he got to sulk about though?"

"Angel," Arowan took Angel in his arms, "you must be the only one who can't see it!"

"See what?"

"He feels like he has been replaced by Mouse this last few days and he's jealous."

"Really?"

"Yes, really."

"Oh ... ok."

"Don't worry, I'll keep an eye out for him and let him know you are worried about him, if I see him."

He squeezed his daughter and signalled to the others that he was ready, once again.

"Keep an eye on Bangus and Trahira."

"I will. And dad?"

"Yes?"

"Be careful."

Arowan smiled at his eldest child and nodded.

So for the second time that day, the hunters made for the tunnel armed with a variety of weapons to ensure a more successful fishing trip this time.

*

Arowan and his friends swam through the turbulent waters where fresh met salty and warily headed out to sea. They went out as far as they dared and having already eaten some Oxystemla, dove down into the depths to fish as quickly as they could.

Adept hunters, they had half filled their nets in no time. There was no second to spare for any games or acrobatic antics, just focussed fishing.

All of them became aware that they were not alone, at the same moment.

And there, slowly emerging from the gloom of the deep, dark sea was the undeniable shape of Inanya.

The men stopped their fishing, stared at her, and half heartedly gripped their spears and pointed them outwards in a defensive motion.

"Please Arowan," said Inanya, "I meant what I said yesterday. And after I saved your lives you still don't trust me?"

"I'm sorry Inanya, old habits die hard, and I wasn't totally convinced that you even believed what you said yesterday."

"I understand it may take some time." Inanya looked hurt, and the two enormous serpents who accompanied her, once again silently applauded her performance.

"We are just fishing quietly as our stocks are low and then we'll be on our way."

"My serpents can help?" She offered.

"Thankyou Inanya, but we're almost done." Arowan went to turn his back on the Serpent Queen and carry on fishing but in a flash of a spiny tail Inanya was inches away from him.

Startled, Arowan stopped in his tracks and stared straight into her dark, soulless eyes, questioning his decision to trust this irrational creature.

"I just need to talk to you for a moment before you go back to Bichir." She explained.

Cautiously he edged away from her penetrating stare so he

could see what was going on around him. He needed to keep his friends in view, he needed to keep watch over Inanya's two slippery companions and more than that he needed to be able to see what Inanya was up to by being a little further away from her, to give him time to react if necessary.

"Ok, what do you want?"

"I would like a favour. In return for helping you yesterday."

"I knew there would be a hidden agenda, a catch to your heroics yesterday."

"This is not just for me Arowan," She whispered silkily, "this would get the girl back to her world."

Now that got Arowan's attention.

"What do you mean?"

I believe that the lost Trident holds the power to get her home. All she has to do is get it."

Arowan laughed a nervous laugh.

"All she has to do is get it!" he said sarcastically, "How on earth is a small girl like Mouse going to find The Trident, let alone make it back to Bichir alive?"

Arowan looked at his friends who were also incredulous at the mere suggestion of such a scheme.

"She is the only one of us who can be away from water for long enough to trek up the volcano and retrieve it for me – I mean – us."

"Hang on a minute..." Inanya's slip of the tongue had not been lost on Arowan, "what do you gain from all this?" He aksed her suspiciously.

"I have the girl's interests at heart but once she's done with it, it could just help me and my serpents too. It will benefit all of us. The girl will get back home. Isn't that what you want Arowan?"

"Yes Inanya, that is what I want and if that is the only way to get her home, it would be amazing, but I still don't understand what you get out of it?"

"Ok, it has long been thought that by just holding The Trident, our curse would be lifted, and it's powers would turn us back into mer-people again, finally."

"Ahhh, there we go. The actual reason you want The Trident. I should have known that your selfish vanity would be behind all this!"

"Not just me Arowan. Me and my serpents are important, obviously, but think of the girl. It may be the only way to get her home. Unless of course you *have* found another way?"

Arowan thought for a moment and swam over to his friends. They huddled close together to discuss Inanya's idea.

Inanya and the two slithery serpents bided their time and let them whisper amongst themselves, barely able to contain their excitement. They were certain of The Tridents powers to lift the curse so they could be mer-people once again but had absolutely no idea if it would get the stupid girl back home. Thanks to Tang they had discovered that no one knew how to get her back to her world, but she was a bargaining tool there were not going to resist using.

Arowan turned back to face them.

"It's too dangerous Inanya. She's a small girl, a human, and she's already encountered the Verzillas twice. She's petrified of them and she wouldn't stand a chance with one of them let alone the herd!"

"I know it's dangerous Arowan but she's fought off dragons before and survived."

"How on earth do you know about *that*?"

"News travels fast around here, everyone in the sea knows about her previous adventure. It seems she gets sent to other worlds for a good reason. This is a good reason Arowan. We will be transformed back to who we should be and we can all live in peace again. I will try to be on good terms with everyone, even like this," she indicated her current form, "but to fit in with the other mer-people, well that would be easier and better for everyone all round."

Inanya stopped herself before she said something she shouldn't. Tang's information had been invaluable but she had to be careful about what she revealed and she didn't want to 'let slip' any knowledge that perhaps everyone wouldn't know.

"She was incredibly brave to have fought the dragon people but at the same time she was scared to death." Arowan replied.

"I'm sure she'll be fine – there's something about her. She looks meek and mild but she is feisty at the same time, I've seen it in her eyes. All we need to do is show her where we assume The Trident to be and give her a few tips to help her on her way. She'll only be gone a couple of hours at the very most."

Arowan had mixed feelings about all this; on the one hand it might be the only way to get Mouse home and he had spent most nights awake trying to work out a plan to do this, not really understanding why she was sent here, but, the thought of sending her on a perilous trip up the side of a recently erupted volcano seemed way too much of a risk.

"I'm not sure about this, I'll have to go back home and ask her." He said.

"Of course." Nodded Inanya.

"We'll return to Bichir when we've filled our nets and discuss this proposition tonight. I'll have an answer for you in the morning."

Frustrated at the wholesomeness of Arowan, she replied "That is the right thing to do." But secretly she was smug inside, she knew the girl would want nothing more than to get back to her world, she would probably do just about anything.

"I'll meet you back here tomorrow when we have reached a decision."

"I'll be here."

And then they were gone as eerily as they had arrived. Murky shapes disappearing into the deep gloomy water.

Arowan and his friends watched them go and at a loss for words, they silently gathered up their half full nets and carried on fishing. They stayed until their nets were full to bursting and swam back to Bichir.

On the way back through the tunnel, they stopped and placed a small amount of the fish in the storage area where it was cool and dark. They would cook it at a later date but for now it would remain fresh until then.

As Arowan lead the way through the rest of the tunnel and back into Bichir, the first person he saw was Mouse. She was sat with Angel and they were quietly sorting out a pile of shells with Bangus and Trahira. He noticed that Bangus was definitely more fascinated by Mouse than the pile of shells, no matter how pretty and colourful they were.

"Here everyone," he called, "some fish for our feast!"

There was a bustle of activity as villagers rushed forward to relieve Arowan and his fellow hunters of the catch.

He was about to go over to Angel when Tang's parents

approached him.

"Arowan, we're worried about Tang."

"Yes, I understand Angel has tried to find him but no one has seen him in a while."

"He's been acting a bit oddly the last couple of days and it's not like him to go anywhere without Angel or the rest of them."

"That's exactly what Angel said. Look, I have something to discuss with everyone when we've eaten and we'll bring this up, see if anyone has heard anything, or if he's said anything. Don't worry, we'll find him." Arowan put a reassuring hand on Tang's mums shoulder and squeezed gently.

Tang's parents smiled weakly and then went to join the others in the preparation of the food.

Angel waited for him to be alone and leapt to her feet and ran over to him.

"A much more successful trip this afternoon then?" She asked.

"Much better."

"And you didn't ..." she looked towards Bangus and Trahira and whispered, "... have any trouble?"

"No Angel, no trouble, but..." He was stopped mid sentence as his other two gangly, web footed children lolloped over and wrapped themselves around him. He looked at Angel over their white heads and mouthed "later."

She nodded and left them to it and returned to where Mouse had remained, sat on the rock, gathering up the shells so they weren't in the way of the feast.

"Everything ok Angel?" Mouse asked as she watched Angel walk towards her with a troubled expression on her face.

"I think so, dad said there was no trouble but was just about to tell me something when those two interrupted." She nodded her head towards Bangus and Trahira who were still enveloped in a hug with their dad.

"Oh. He wasn't hurt was he?"

"I couldn't see anything obvious, so I don't think so."

"And the others all look ok too."

"Yeah, let's hope so. Now let's get these shells back to my dwelling and get back here to help with the food."

Angel and Mouse scooped up the shells and carried them back to Angel's cave room, which Mouse had to admit, looked better than it did before the volcanic eruption. The few larger rocks which had been arranged in a near semi circle had juddered their way across the ground and positioned themselves nearer the walls which made the area seem more spacious. All Angel had to do was replace some of the shells on the wall and it would be as good as new. Mouse had already decided on a design for some of the shells, something that Angel would remember her by, when she eventually found a way to get back home.

They tidied up the room quickly and then ran back down to the beach where the familiar gathering had begun.

Mouse spotted Arowan busily getting the fire going which was just in time because the light was beginning to fade. The fiery bowls were being strategically placed around the beach area to give more light and apart from the slightly troubled look on Arowan's face, the whole lagoon looked magical.

The light from the main fire and the twinkling lights from the bowls were dancing in the dusky evening, and the lagoon lit up by firelight cast different depths of blue across the surface of the motionless pool.

There were no vine leaves tonight, just an enormous amount of freshly roasted fish, an assortment of leaves and plenty of juicy berries.

The chatter was relaxed and steady while the food was being eaten, the past few days forgotten for a while. The conversation was more about the children, their daily activities and how good the food was.

No one noticed Arowan as he slowly walked up to his platform and silently watched, with a small smile, his friends and family.

"Everyone!" He shouted above the hum of conversation.

Silence immediately engulfed the lagoon except for the constant drumming of water from the fall at the other end of the cave.

All the big pale blue eyes focussed on Arowan.

"I have something to tell you." The silence ended as the villagers looked at each other and mumbled their confusion.

"Calm down, please."

Arowan waited for their attention once again.

"When we went fishing, the second time today, we met with Inanya and her serpents."

Gasps and shocked expressions.

"I can assure you, sssshhhh, there was no trouble."

"Then what dad?" Asked Angel.

"I'm trying to tell you all, so please, let me tell you what happened and then we will need to have a discussion."

There was a bit of 'sshhhing' and then there was quiet.

"Thankyou. Now I know these past few days have been difficult to say the least, and the unexpected arrival of Mouse, who feels like part of our large family now, has

134

thrown us into some confusion .... but we now have a decision to make which will affect us all, massively."

Arowan watched the villagers take this in, but could see they were desperate to know what he meant.

"So, we met with Inanya, there was no trouble at all but she did have an interesting proposition for us. Well, for one of us in particular, actually."

Arowan looked directly at Mouse.

All the white heads followed suit, and they all looked at Mouse.

"Me?" She squeaked.

"Yes, you Mouse."

"What is it Arowan?"

"Before I tell you, all of you, we have to consider the consequences of such a request and it will be a hard decision to make. But, it's one only Mouse can make ultimately."

"Dad what on earth is it?" Pleaded Angel, half wanting to know and half not. She knew that anything involving Inanya would be fraught with danger but she also knew that her dad would not be discussing this with everyone if he was absolutely certain it would end badly.

Arowan explained the conversation between him and the Serpent Queen, and waited for a response. But unusually the villagers had lost their voices. An unheard of phenomenon.

There were several open mouths.

There were several bowed heads.

And there were two very horrified faces that stood out, Angel and Mouse.

"What did you say dad?" Asked Angel in a shaky voice.

"I said I would discuss it with everyone, especially you

Mouse," he looked at her sincerely, "and then I would meet her in the morning with an answer."

"You have to say no, there *must* be another way to get Mouse home!"

"That's what we need to discuss Angel."

"What if it is ... the only way I mean Arowan?" Asked Mouse.

Arowan and Angel looked at Mouse, who all of a sudden seemed smaller.

"I mean, this is the first time since I have been here that there has been *any* suggestion of getting me home."

"There must be another way Mouse." Said Angel as she searched her dad's face for confirmation.

Mouse looked at Arowan, waiting for a positive response but she feared he might not have an alternative option.

"That's the problem girls ... I just don't know." So with his head bowed, he left Angel and Mouse to discuss this unique situation with the rest of the villagers. As he walked away from them he turned and watched them stroll slowly to the water and wade in. He looked on as they swam to the centre of the pool, two lone figures not saying a word to each other.

He conversed with the villagers who were all in agreement by the time the girls, sometime later, got out of the water.

Angel and Mouse wandered over to Arowan and the remaining villagers, most of the youngsters were tucked up on their stony beds in their soft, wet blankets by now.

"Mouse," said Arowan, "we are all in agreement about this. We are all very worried that you are very young and a decision like this is too much for you to take on."

He motioned for the girls to come closer, and he put his long arms around them both. As Mouse returned the much needed hug her hand brushed against Arowan's fin, it felt delicate and silky. A brief reminder of why these people could not do this themselves, why it was down to her. Only *she* could trek through the jungle and climb the volcano and go that long without the need to be near water. If Inanya was transformed back to a mermaid, their lives would be more harmonious and trouble free.

"It's ok Arowan," she said, "I think I know what I have to do."

"Mouse!" Shrieked Angel, "You can't do it, it's far too dangerous."

"I just need to see Inanya for myself and make sure I see that she means it when she says that she'll be good if I do go and get The Trident."

"But what if she lies to you?"

"I just have to see her Angel, then I'll decide."

Arowan marvelled at the level headedness of this 12 year old girl who had entered their lives so suddenly and could change their lives for the better. He couldn't comprehend the strength of character she possessed and he undeniably applauded her courage and determination.

"We'll go and meet her in the morning Mouse," He said, "but I suggest we all get some sleep for now."

The concerned faces of all the villagers smiled in Mouse's direction, but before they dispersed Arowan had one last thing to say.

"We must all keep an eye out for Tang, if anyone hears anything, or knows anything about where he might be, come to me. I'm sure he's testing himself, and us in a way, on a little adventure of his own but let's not forget he's only young too."

There were murmurs of agreement and then everyone

disappeared in various directions; some to the pool for their final swim and some to their dwellings so settle down for the night.

Arowan squeezed the girls, plonked a kiss on top of both their heads and left them alone on the beach.

Angel and Mouse sat on some rocks by the water's edge and watched everyone finish swimming and leave them to it. They were soon the only ones not tucked up in bed and Bichir seemed ghostly quiet. Even the sound of the waterfall seemed hushed this late at night.

"Angel, can I ask you something?" Asked Mouse.

"Of course."

"What happened to your mum?"

Angel looked to the ground with big sad eyes and then up at Mouse.

"Inanya killed her because she was more beautiful than her."

"How, I mean why her?"

"It was an unfortunate set of events really but my mum didn't stand a chance."

"Inanya caught her and killed her?" Asked Mouse warily.

"Pretty much. My mum could also sing, she had a lovely voice, and she used to sing to me, Bangus and Trahira before we went to sleep every night, soft lullabys which soothed us and helped us drift off. Well one day she was out in the ocean, gathering some large shells, singing happily, and she was on her way to the surface for some Oxystemla when she was attacked by Inanya and her serpents before she could take some. She had been with some friends but they weren't quick enough to keep up with the serpents. All they heard was Inanya screaming about my mum's voice and that it should be her that could sing while the sun shone down on her skin. They dragged her down and down and she drowned before they could hurt her."

Angels eyes had filled with huge tears and Mouse moved to cuddle her distraught friend.

"I'm so so sorry Angel, that's so cruel."

"Her friends have struggled to get over it, that they couldn't get to her in time."

"I can imagine, but we all know how bad the serpents and Inanya can be, they wouldn't have been able to change a thing."

"I know, and it took them a long time to realise it, but they are a lot better now."

"How long ago was it?"

"It was about 6 years ago when Trahira was only little. She doesn't remember much about mum at all which is a shame."

"Does Bangus remember much?"

"More than Trahira but not a whole lot."

"But you remember everything." Said Mouse as she squeezed Angel in a big hug.

"Yes, and so does dad. I know he thinks this change of heart from Inanya is dodgy but he's trying to do his best for everyone."

"He's a good dad."

They sat and chatted for a while, avoiding tomorrow's big decision, and then meandered back to Angel's dwelling, and to bed.

*

As he regained consciousness he realised that his head hurt and his inevitably broken bones screamed in silent agony. He didn't know where he was, and he could only see out of one eye, and the shafts of light streaming through the tall jungle trees was fading.

He seemed to be half in and half out of water but unable to move regardless.

He coughed and bright red blood gurgled in his throat and spilled down the side of his pale face. Tears sprang to his eyes as the motion of coughing restricted his breathing and sent stabbing pains across his chest. He knew that if he survived this, it would be a miracle.

***

<u>Chapter Eight</u>

Mouse and Angel sauntered to the beach area where most of the villagers had already come together. The breakfast was being prepared amidst apprehensive chatter, and when they noticed the arrival of Mouse, all eyes were upon her.

Genuine smiles and open arms greeted Mouse, all of them having come to accept her as one of their own, and all of them extremely anxious about what lay ahead for her.

Arowan joined them on the large rock where the two girls were sat.

"Morning you two." He said.

"Morning dad."

"Morning Arowan."

"So Mouse, have you had enough time to consider Inanya's request?" Asked Arowan.

The whole of Bichir fell silent.

"Um, yes Arowan, I have."

"You don't have to do it Mouse, you know that don't you?"

"Yes I know. But if it's the only way to get me home, then I have to try."

There were gasps and saddened expressions from all around her; shock that such a small girl was prepared to take on such a task, and sadness for the danger she could encounter.

"I'm annoyed that I haven't even been able to think of another way to get you home Mouse, and even more annoyed that this might be the only way."

"It's ok Arowan, but if it *is* the only way, I have to try."

"You're a very brave, very grown up young lady," Arowan smiled fondly at her, "now eat your breakfast and we'll go and meet Inanya and see what she has to say about the location of The Trident."

"Ok Arowan."

Mouse and Angel were handed bowls of berries and cups of water which they munched through slowly, each of them deep in thought about the meeting with Inanya and her horrible serpents.

"Do you think things will be better once she's turned back into a mer-maid Angel?"

Angel thought for a moment before replying.

"Well I hope so. Most of the trouble we have had with her and her ancestors has been to do with greed and jealousy. Once she's a mer-maid again she'll be able to live in a normal village under the sea, one which isn't at the bottom of the ocean where it's dark and gloomy."

"But she's *sooo* bad, will becoming a beautiful mer-maid really change her *that* much?"

"I really don't know Mouse but I hope so. She's the only

one who causes trouble for us and the mer-people. It would be nice to all live in peace."

"But what about those other creatures, the ones who attacked Arowan and his friends?"

"The serpillions?"

"Yes, won't they still be the same, won't they still cause trouble?"

"To be honest Mouse, I've never even seen one!"

"Really?"

"Yes, really. I think my dad has seen them once before but they are usually night hunters and they live in the depths, somewhere we hardly ever go, so encounters are rare."

"I wonder why they were so near the other day then?"

"I don't know but dad and his friends were lucky Inanya was about that day otherwise they wouldn't have come home."

There was a pause in the conversation whilst the two girls digested that last sentence, neither of them wishing to dwell on what could have happened.

"Mmm, maybe she will be ok then, once she's changed, I mean." Said Mouse, trying to be positive.

"Let's hope so."

"Ok, well I've finished mine," Mouse held out her empty bowl, "shall we have a quick swim and then get ready to go?"

"Good idea."

The girls rinsed out their bowls in the water and stacked them neatly back where they were all stored in a small recess in the rocky wall, and then ran and splashed their way into the pool.

They were quickly joined by Bonito, Vimba and Mora and although they tried frivolity, their hearts were just not in it.

When they had all stopped and were at the edge of the water, they all turned to face the beach where Arowan and the villagers were deep in conversation.

"One guess as to what they're talking about!" Exclaimed Bonito.

"Guess that'll be me." Said Mouse with half a smile.

"I think you're right Mouse," Bonito replied, "are you really going to find the lost Trident?"

"Looks like it."

"Are you scared?"

"A bit."

"I would be too but I'm sure you'll be ok. There's no evil dragons to fight this time." Bonito said, trying desperately to lighten the mood.

Mouse looked at him and knew he was trying to help, "But there will be Verzillas instead."

The four friends looked at each other with understanding, and then at Mouse.

"C'mon Mouse, let's get out of the water and see what they have planned." Suggested Angel as she nodded her head towards the villagers on the beach.

"Good idea Angel, and Mouse," said Vimba, "we'll help in any way we can."

The other friends all agreed and gave Mouse some wet, watery hugs.

"Thanks, I think I'll need all the help I can get."

With that, they all swam back to the beach to find out exactly what was being discussed.

Surprisingly Mouse wasn't the name they heard being talked about.

It was Tang.

Tang's parents were justifiably worried about him as no

one had seen him for ages.

As Mouse, Angel and the other friends listened in, they understood that there would be a full scale search once Mouse had left for The Trident.

Tangs parents were being comforted by a number of villagers, all scared for Tang's well being. The unexplained disappearance of a villager, especially a youngster, was rare. And unfortunately when someone had gone missing it had never ended well, which was undeniably in the back of everyone's minds at that moment.

Remarkably Tang's parents put aside their own fear and approached Mouse.

"We both hope you get back safely to us Mouse," said Tang's dad, "it's a very brave thing you're doing."

"Thankyou, hopefully it'll be ok and Inanya won't be mean to any of you, any more."

Tang's parents each gave her a hug, said a quiet, "Good luck," and slowly meandered back to their dwelling.

Angel and her friends were chatting amongst themselves, about where they could imagine Tang being for all this time. But Mouse wasn't listening, she was thinking about her own mum and dad, the only comfort being that at least they wouldn't be worried about where she was, knowing that time virtually stood still when she was transported to other worlds.

Startled from her thoughts as Arowan put a hand on her shoulder, Mouse knew that she had to concentrate on where she was now, and what she was about to do.

"Are you ready to go Mouse?" Asked Arowan.

"I think so."

"We have plenty of Oxystemla and we all have weapons ... just in case."

"Ok." Mouse stood up and Angel joined her.

"Bangus and Trahira are being looked after for as long as necessary but I'm still not sure about you coming with us Angel." Said Arowan.

"You're not going without me, and besides I know the jungle better than anyone, and I want to see what Inanya says about the location of The Trident and work out if there's an easy way to get to it or not." Argued Angel, defiantly.

"Ok, I s'pose knowing the immediate area will help a little but none of us knows what's beyond."

Mouse noticed their concerned expressions but already knew that she would be on her own for most of the trek.

"C'mon, let's get it over with, we'll listen to what she has to say and then we can plan the next course of action ourselves." Said Arowan.

With that Arowan and his four strongest hunters grabbed their weapons, checked their pouches were secure and walked towards the tunnel. Angel and Mouse said their goodbyes to their friends and followed behind.

Mouse still didn't like the tunnel but she was getting used to it, and thankfully before long the tunnel was behind them and they were swimming down the river with the warm sun on their faces, approaching the large rock where they would all consume some Oxystemla. They sat in silence while the magical little plant was handed around, each one of them taking a small piece and then one by one, plopping back into the water.

They followed the river to the sea and swam out to the depths, the dark water that Inanya was so desperately trying to escape from.

Arowan and his friends waited for Angel and Mouse to

catch up, the two girls had fallen behind where the river and sea met and the turbulent waters caused even the strongest swimmer, to need a few more ounces of energy to overcome the water's power.

Once they were all together, with a quick but deliberate nod at Mouse, Arowan instructed them to dive.

Mouse and Angel followed the five men as they lead the way to the meeting place.

Although fearful, Mouse watched the men swimming ahead and marvelled at their grace, and the colours of their fins as the water rippled over them with each movement of their lithe bodies. But the sunlight from above was fading fast as they swam deeper and deeper into the dark world where the Serpent Queen resided.

The five men came to a halt, weaponry poised and ready for whatever may happen next. Arowan motioned to Angel and Mouse to move into the middle of them and the men formed a protective circle around them both. All seven pairs of eyes were wildly darting about in all directions, searching for the first glimpse of Inanya herself. They didn't have to wait long.

A flash of orange and white streaked passed them, followed by another, and another. They formed a squirming mass a few feet away from them.

"Stay alert!" Shouted Arowan and weapons were gripped tighter and pointed outwards.

The serpents came to a halt in front of the wary group and slowly, behind them, loomed the unmistakable shape of Inanya; jet black hair almost slithering around her face, her long spiny tail propelling her through the murky water and her evil eyes focussed completely on Mouse, who was trying to hide behind one of Arowan's friends.

And although it was impossible, Mouse was sure she felt the water chill just that little bit more, just in the Serpent Queen's presence.

"Arowan. Mouse." She purred through a wide, toothy grin.

"Inanya." Replied Arowan.

"I see you were able to convince the girl that this needed to be done." Inanya never took her eyes off Mouse.

"She hasn't decided anything yet," replied Arowan, "we've just come to find out what you have to say, to see how dangerous this is for her and to see if you really know the location of The Trident."

"I see." A flicker of rage sparked in her eyes for a brief moment before she composed herself and waited for Arowan to continue.

"We have to know – without doubt – the exact place Mouse will need to go, in order to plan the safest route. If you are in any doubt Inanya, Mouse will not be going anywhere."

"Arowan, the location of The Trident has been passed down in my family for generations. Now lower your weapons and let's get this over with."

Arowan's friends looked to him for guidance and he took a moment to consider the request, then nodded to them to comply.

Weapons lowered, Inanya moved in closer.

Mouse was able to study her up close, from behind Arowan's friend of course. She studied Inanya's grey sallow face with piercing dark eyes, the shiny black hair which had a life of it's own, like a million shiny black eels crowning her head, her greenish/grey torso which looked like she should have been dead for a hundred years, and

148

then there was her tail ... black, spikey and dangerous.

An exact replica - a live version of her transformed picture. And although Mouse remembered her feelings when she saw the picture for the first time, it was nothing compared to the reality of such a creature.

"Ok, tell me where The Trident can be found." Arowan finally asked.

"If we drop to the seabed, I can show you, it'll be easier that way."

"Ok, but I'm watching you Inanya, no funny business."

The three serpents went first, followed by Inanya and then Arowan, the girls and his friends.

Once down on the seabed Inanya began picking out rocks and laying them flat on the sand at first and then she built up one end by carefully piling rocks on top of one another. Eventually she had finished.

"This," she said, "is the edge of the jungle which runs alongside the beach."

"Ok." Said Arowan.

"And here," she pointed to a larger rock, "is where Bichir is. Now, just passed the tunnel you use every day, which comes out into the river, there is a second tunnel." She pointed a grey, bony hand just passed the rock which represented Bichir.

"I never knew there was another tunnel, are you sure Inanya?" Questioned Arowan.

"It's there. It may be less obvious as no one uses it on a daily basis, but it is there all the same," she glared at Arowan, "it's a similar size and a bit longer but it comes out just at the base of the volcano."

Inanya glanced around at everyone to make sure they were all following, and once satisfied that she could continue, she pointed to a rock which was placed at the bottom of the pile she'd constructed earlier.

"Now this is where you'll come out of the tunnel but it's a fair distance between there and the best way to get up the side of the volcano so you will have to follow the base of it round to the East until you come across an area which looks like a gravesite."

Mouse looked at Arowan with wide, horrified eyes.

"What do you mean, a gravesite, Inanya?" Arowan asked, seeing the shock on Mouse's small face.

"It's nothing to be scared of," she replied, "it's just an area where the mer-people buried their families and erected beautiful shell shaped stones in their honour."

Arowan carried on watching Mouse to see her reaction, and thankfully her face had softened slightly.

"So all I will see is lots of stone shells?" Mouse asked the Serpent Queen in a small voice as she peeked around Arowan's friend to look Inanya straight in the eye.

"Yes. They probably don't look much now after all these years but that's all they are." Inanya looked at Arowan for confirmation that she could proceed.

Arowan nodded.

"So ... once you reach the grave – I mean – the shells, if you look up the side of the volcano there will be a sort of path, again, it won't be obvious after all this time, but there will be stone slabs and a trail etched out of the rock."

"What if it's not there, or if it's all overgrown by now? How will Mouse find it?" Angel asked, "I've been to the bottom of the volcano loads of times and I've never seen a path."

"Hang on," said Arowan, "what do you mean you've been to the bottom of the volcano young lady?" He stared accusingly at Angel.

"We all have dad," said Angel, realising her mistake, "it's not that far, honestly."

"The path is way too far around to the East for you to ever get to." Interupted Inanya impatiently.

"Don't think I'll forget about this." Threatened Arowan as he continued to glare at Angel.

"I've been there, we all have." Hissed Angel, baring all of her little sharp teeth at Inanya.

"Anyway," said Inanya, ignoring Angel and regaining control of the situation, "I'm sure you will find the path, it was carved into the rock thousands of years ago, it will still be there."

"Is Mouse to follow this path then, *if* she can find it?" Asked Angel.

"Yes, it climbs up the side of the volcano in a zigzag pattern. It's the path my ancestors, our ancestors Arowan, took whenever the king wanted to address his people. They used it as a sort of guide to organise the queue of mer-people wishing to gather together all at once. They all swam along the path to the meeting place, where the king would then appear in front of the Cave of Thrones with The Trident."

"So The Trident is just up the path and inside the cave?" Asked Angel, curiosity having gotten the better of her.

"Well, probably not just inside, there may be an inner chamber where it, and other royal treasures were kept."

"Other treasures?" Asked one of Arowan's friends.

"I've no idea if they are all still there, I just want – *we* just want," She corrected "The Trident." She was losing her patience and her tail swished through the water rapidly.

"Ok, let's calm down," said Arowan as he noticed the

Queens serpents getting agitated as well as Inanya, "we need a moment to go to the surface, take some Oxystemla and discuss your plan."

"Go ahead." Replied Inanya.

Arowan thought she looked relieved to be left alone for a moment so he motioned for the others to follow him up to the surface.

Pure joy at feeling the sun on their faces, the seven of them took in great gulps of fresh air as if to cleanse themselves of the murky, dark water below.

They nibbled on some Oxystemla whilst treading water and bobbing up and down.

"Young lady," said Arowan as he turned to Angel, "seeing as you've been to the bottom of the volcano, you can tell us if this scheme of Inanya's is feasible?"

"It is, but obviously I don't know anything about a hidden path as it starts much further round than I could ever get to."

"Mouse."

"Yes Arowan?"

"How do you feel about it now you know how far it is, and what Inanya is expecting of you?"

"It seems ok to me," said Mouse as she shivered in the water, "but that's without any scary, hungry beasts trying to eat me!"

"Well that is what you have to consider; not only do you have to get The Trident and remain in one piece, you have to get all the way back to Bichir with it too!"

"We'll make sure you have plenty of weapons Mouse," Added Angel, "I only wish I could go with you." She gently pulled Mouse into a cold, wet hug.

"We can all go some of the way with Mouse," said

Arowan, "but the trek around and up the mountain will be impossible for us."

"It's ok, I'm used to mountains, hiding and danger!" Reassured Mouse, although truthfully, she wasn't reassured at all.

"So," said Arowan, "the question is Mouse, will you go ahead with this?"

"If you think you will have a happier, more peaceful life when she's back to being a nice mer-maid, then yes, I'll give it a try."

"Nothing is guaranteed Mouse but it couldn't be any worse than the last few days."

"That's settled then, I'll go."

"Ok, let's get back down to Inanya and tell her."

Mouse did notice a few worried glances pass between Arowan's friends before they all dove back down to meet up again with the Serpent Queen.

As they approached, Inanya and her serpents were huddled together in a swirling mass of slippery tails and slithery bodies.

Mouse shuddered at the very sight of them. She would not being doing this task for them, she would be doing it for Angel and Bichir and possibly, hopefully, for herself.

"Ah Arowan," said Inanya, her voice trying to ooze charm, "so have you made a decision?" She looked straight at Mouse.

"The decision was entirely Mouse's to make, and she has said she'll give it a go." Explained Arowan.

"Splendid! When will you go?" Shrieked Inanya as she clasped her long, bony hands together with glee and satisfaction."She will go tomorrow Inanya," answered Arowan, "we have a more pressing situation to deal with first."

"A situation more pressing than this?"

"One of the villagers has gone missing and we're all going out to look for him once we return from this meeting today."

Mouse and Angel didn't miss the tension which seemed to overcome Inanya and her serpents.

"What have you done to Tang?" Mouse blurted out and swam towards Inanya, anger overpowering fear for a moment.

Inanya feigned shock at such a preposterous accusation, her serpents writhing in fury around her.

"I truly don't know what you mean young girl!" She looked at Arowan with the most innocent expression she could manage.

"Mouse?" Arowan quizzed, "What makes you say that?"

"She's up to something, I'm sure." Mouse had now retreated back to the protection of her group.

"Like what?"

"I – I – I don't know how to describe it but I have a feeling that she knows what happened to Tang."

"Me too." Said Angel.

Arowan looked Inanya in the eye. Inanya who was trying her hardest to remain calm. Inanya who needed to get away from here as quickly as possible before she exploded with rage!

"And do you Inanya, do you know what has happened to Tang?"

"Of course I don't, I just reacted to the news knowing what would come next. I knew you would all think I had something to do with it but I meant what I said, I'm really trying to build bridges Arowan, why would I do something to jeopardise that, especially when I need your help at the moment?" She couldn't help her tail flicking to and fro due to the heightened emotions of the moment. She hoped she'd acted well enough to pull this one off.

"Ok," said Arowan, "you have a point. Time will tell though Inanya, and I'd better not find out you have had anything to do with the disappearance of Tang. We will prepare Mouse for her journey tomorrow and if she's successful, we'll return here the day after tomorrow, first thing."

"Ok Arowan, I'll be here," Inanya stared straight at Mouse, "be careful with The Trident girl, it's very powerful."

Mouse wanted to poke out her tongue at the horrible queen but instead she grabbed Angel's long fingered, webbed hand and swam up to the surface.

They were soon joined by Arowan and his four friends, and once again they relished the warmth of the sun on their skin and the brightness of such a lovely day.

"Is everyone ok?" Asked Arowan.

All six heads nodded.

"Let's go home then."

The seven of them took a more leisurely swim back to Bichir, all the while keeping their eyes peeled for any sign of Tang.

With no sightings and heavy hearts they swam back through the tunnel and into Bichir. Most of the villagers were on the beach area, all deep in conversation, some were discussing Mouse's trek but mostly the chatter was about the search for Tang.

Expectant faces greeted them, when they were spotted, and they made their way into the crowd.

"It's all agreed," said Arowan, "Mouse will go tomorrow."

There were several 'ahhhs', some muttering from the villagers and some shocked faces. Mouse could feel the warmth and comfort from these strange gangly people she had come to love, and knew that they would be worried about her safety all the while she was gone.

She was deep in thought when she felt a little pat on her leg. Mouse looked down at the little white headed youngster, and the little boy looked up at her with the same big, pale blue eyes as Angel, and he held out his hand. In the little palm was a string of coloured shells.

Mouse knelt down to the little boys level and took the shells.

"Wow, they're lovely." She said.

"They're for you, for luck." Said the boy, who could only have been about 6 years old.

"Oh thankyou," said Mouse as she hugged the boy, "I'll take them with me tomorrow."

The boy moved back to his parents who both beamed with pride at their offspring.

"Ok," interrupted Arowan, "we'll discuss how to help Mouse later on, but now we have to plan a search party."

"We'll just go for a quick swim, get this sea water off us, and then we'll help dad." Said Angel.

"Ok."

So Angel and Mouse ran and jumped into the cool fresh water.

As they swam, Arowan organised the villagers into groups for the search, each group having a strong hunter for protection and a couple of larger villagers to help carry Tang back, if he was found.

By the time Angel and Mouse waded out of the water, all of the villagers going on the search had been for a quick swim and were waiting for the 'go ahead' from Arowan. They were both in Arowan's group and their area to search was up the river towards the volcano. So whilst their priority would be searching for Tang they would also be able to have a look for the second tunnel.

Arowan was certain that there wasn't one so this would be a chance to confirm Inanya's knowledge on the locations of landmarks she had told Mouse to look for.

"Ok everyone, let's go! Be alert, be careful and stay together in your groups. Once you've searched your designated area return to Bichir."

So with a bustle of anticipation and hope, some of the villagers of Bichir filtered towards the tunnel, some swam towards the waterfall, some out into the jungle and some had an equally important job of staying behind to look after the youngsters and keeping them occupied.

Arowan, Angel, Mouse and the rest of their group followed the other searchers through the tunnel and then veered off to the right, up river. The group consisted of Arowan, Angel, Mouse and three large male villagers; plenty of 'muscle' to carry someone back home if needed.

They stayed close together as they swam slowly against the natural flow of the water, eyes peeled for any hint of an unknown tunnel or a suggestion of someone having been that way recently.

Every so often Arowan or one of the other men would investigate the riverbank where a gap in the dense undergrowth presented a possibility, or an unknown downtrodden patch of grass indicated previous activity.

They had searched for nearly an hour but no matter how hard they looked they could not find Tang. They also could not find the second tunnel.

"Here!" Shouted one of the men, just as they were nearing the rounded part of the river where the unsuccessful fishing trip had taken place not so long ago.

As the others got closer they noticed the ground had definitely been disturbed, on the right hand side of the river. The group hauled themselves up onto land and had a scout around the immediate area. They were all acutely aware that this was on the outskirts of Verzilla territory.

So keeping close together they were encouraged to see that someone had been here recently, and the disturbed foliage didn't look devastated enough for it to have been a large beast. So with wary movement and weapons poised, they ventured further into the jungle.

They brushed the large tropical plants aside, pulled the long grasses apart but no sign of Tang. None of them dared go much further as they were getting too close to the trees and any manner of danger could be lurking only feet away, and avoiding disaster would be impossible.

"Dad?"

"Yes Angel."

"This is hopeless, where could he be?"

"I honestly don't know, but let's just hope that one of the other groups have been more successful."

"What's that?" All eyes turned to Mouse as she pointed towards the trees.

"What is it?" Asked one of the men.

"There's a sort of path, look, through there, between the trees." Replied Mouse.

"Wait!" Hissed Arowan as everyone else looked to be making their way towards where Mouse had been pointing.

They stopped.

"What dad?"

"Just wait a minute, we need to be ready for anything. We have no idea what may be watching us from those trees." The men formed a protective circle around Angel and Mouse and with weapons held out in front of them, inched forward slowly.

They edged forward slowly and carefully so as not to alert anyone, or anything, to their presence in the jungle.

The little shuffling group reached the path and saw immediately what it lead to.

The second tunnel!

The path was clearly used often as the grasses failed to grow on it but what or who used this path was something none of them wanted to dwell on.

It wasn't a long pathway – probably twice as long as Arowan if he lay down – which then disappeared into the ground as it sloped downwards into the newly discovered tunnel which looked pretty much the same as the one they used every day to get to Bichir.

"Well, we found the tunnel." Whispered Mouse.

"But not Tang." Sighed Angel.

"Ssshhh!" Signalled Arowan, and at once him and the men were back on full alert, knives gripped and pointed outwards.

SNAP!

The startling noise seemed to echo around the jungle.

Something was watching them, and that something wasn't far away.

"Keep close together and slowly move back towards the river." Arowan whispered, and the group began to inch their way backwards, the way they had come, with wide searching eyes and their ears listening out for any further unexpected noises.

Whatever was out there seemed to be moving with them; the nearer to the river they got, the nearer the snapping of twigs got.

Angel let out an ear piercing shriek!

And then everything went from slow motion to fast forward.

The beady eyed Verzilla had showed itself, Angel had screamed and crashed backwards into the others.

There was the briefest moment of silence and absolute stillness.

Just a brief moment.

Then everything happened at once.

The Verzilla leapt forward, it's huge heavy body thumping at the ground as it went.

Arowan and his little search party watched the first split second of it lurching towards them and then turned their backs on it and ran for their lives.

Thurump thurump.

The snarling beast, defying it's weight restriction, was catching them up, and fast!

Arowan practically picked up Angel and Mouse as he powered through to the front of the group.

Thurump thurump.

They could feel the ground shake and smell the laboured vile breath of the Verzilla as it chased after them.

The river was in sight, only a few more moments...

Thurump thurump.

The group kept running as fast as their legs would carry them and then with a giant leap off the riverbank, they all hit the water with several large splashes!

As they rose to the surface individually, all of them turned to face the bank, where a large angry Verzilla was gnashing his teeth together, strings of drool dripping from his jaws, his feet pounding the ground at the very spot where they had leapt to safety.

Short of breath they stared at it triumphantly. Whoops of joy and relief from all of them.

The Verzilla continued to stomp and stare at them in the outside hope that one of them would float close enough for him to snare his dinner.

Thankfully the group were now in the middle of the river being carried by the flow of the water and heading back towards Bichir.

And so, as they looked behind them they could see the Verzilla admit defeat and thump his way back into the depths of the jungle.

Wearily they swam into the tunnel and trudged back onto the beach area where several other groups had already arrived.

No sign of Tang from any of them.

Breathless they joined the others and everyone swapped stories of what they had, or hadn't, come across.

They all sat on the beach and waited for all the other groups to return, and return they did, no one having found Tang.

So with a sombre atmosphere, some went for a swim, some went to prepare the evening feast and some just remained on the beach, deep in thought.

A lot had happened in Bichir in the last week. Their normal day to day lives had been in turmoil and everyone knew that they had a few more days to endure, without really knowing whether or not the outcome would be a positive one.

The evening was spent going through the events of the day and the plans for tomorrow, and although the conversation flowed easily there was a serious undertone to everything that was said.

There was no frolicking in the water, just gentle swims. There was no laughter, just the occasional smile. And by the end of the evening everyone felt emotionally drained.

Arowan bade the girls goodnight and ushered Bangus and Trahira into their dwelling for the night. Angel and Mouse strolled back to Angel's dwelling chatting over the plans for tomorrow as they went.

"Are you going to be able to sleep tonight Mouse?" Asked Angel.

"I have no idea but I'll have to try."

"I don't think I'd be able to."

"Well if I'm going to need to be alert for tomorrow then I hope I get a few hours at least."

"Are you scared Mouse?"

Mouse looked at her beautiful new friend and nodded. Angel put her long arm around Mouse and hugged her tight.

"You'll be ok."

"Mmm."

"My dad will go as far as he can with you, probably to the other end of the tunnel we found today, so at least you'll have some protection for some of the way."

"Then I'm on my own."

"We'll make sure you have weapons and it's not like you haven't had to use them before."

"I know but that was unexpected, I just reacted to the situation. This will almost be like knowing that I'll have to use them."

"But that's good in a way Mouse, you'll be prepared and ready for it this time."

"I suppose."

It didn't matter how reassuring Angel was trying to be, Mouse just couldn't shake off the feeling of impending dangers.

They got themselves as comfy as possible for the night and without further conversation, each drifted off into an unsettled nights' sleep.

***

<u>Chapter Nine</u>

The morning started bright and early with an abnormal tension in the air, although everyone was trying their hardest to hide it.

Angel and Mouse got themselves ready, had a quick swim and meandered onto the beach where, it seemed, everyone else already was.

They were greeted by nervous smiles and gentle reassuring pats on their shoulders, as they walked through the crowd to where Arowan was waiting.

"Morning girls."

"Morning dad."

"Hi Arowan."

"Let's get you a drink and some fruits before we start on planning the day and possible eventualities, see if we can relax a bit first." He suggested.

Before they could reply bowls of fruit and cups of drinks were produced and thrust into their hands, by caring and concerned villagers trying to do anything to help. And after some nervous bustling about everyone on the beach seemed to take a breath and relax just a little bit, all of them seated on and around the beach area, chatting in various groups.

Mouse sat deep in thought, twiddling with the bracelet Angel had given her and the string of shells she had been handed yesterday.

Shells...

Grave sites ...

Verzillas ...

Was she really brave enough to do this - alone?

Her troubled contemplation was broken when a large webbed hand rested on her shoulder. She looked up at Arowan as he said "It's time to get ready Mouse."

"Oh. Ok Arowan."

"I got up early to get a few easy to carry weapons and other bits you may need."

"Thanks. So what have I got?"

Almost the entire population of Bichir leaned in to see what Arowan had prepared for Mouse. He bent down and picked up a small bag, a larger version of the pouches used for carrying the Oxystemla, and began to show everyone what he had chosen.

In the bag were a couple of knives, a pouch of Oxystemla, a pouch of water, some sharpened twigs and some small rocks.

There were murmurs of approval all around.

"I get what most of it is for Arowan but why the Oxystemla?"

"Well," he said cautiously, "it's just in case you do come across a Verzilla and the Oxystemla may work in the same way as it did on the injured beast the other day, you remember, it put it into a trance?"

"Yes, I remember."

"So if you find yourself in a *situation*, this might be worth a try."

"Good idea dad." Interrupted Angel.

"And if that doesn't work stab it with your knife!" Bangus butted in and made a stabbing motion with his arm.

"Or throw rocks at it!" Squealed Trahira.

Mouse couldn't help but smile at their enthusiasm and their innocent understanding of the treacherous situation.

Arowan put his arm around his smallest children and decided that here, in front of all the youngsters, was not the place to go through battle tactics with Mouse. He was glad they didn't comprehend the severity of what lay ahead and didn't want to scare them by showing Mouse what she had to do if she ran into danger.

"Right," he announced, "let's get Mouse ready to go and I'll go through the rest once we've left."

The next fifteen minutes was spent hugging everyone and accepting their wishes of good luck.

Arowan had allowed Angel to come to the river but no further, not after yesterday's trauma.

Eventually Arowan, Angel, Mouse and five large villagers left Bichir, filled with dread and fear but also a tiny bit of hope.

Once through the tunnel, they swam up river to a clearing in the jungle not far from Bichir. They all clambered up the bank and waited for Arowan's further instructions.

"Ok Mouse, we'll try to get you as prepared as best we can. Firstly, we'll do some defensive lessons and then we'll sit down and go over your route."

"Ok Arowan."

"Do I get to stay for this bit dad?"

"Yes Angel, then straight back to Bichir."

Arowan and the other five men proceeded to re-enact various scenarios for Mouse, some defensive and some attacking. Mouse watched every move trying to imagine herself having to use them. Or hopefully, not having to use them.

"Ok Mouse," said Arowan, "you've watched us play fight, now it's your turn."

"Um ... now?"

"Never a better time." Arowan smiled fondly at her.

"Yes. Ok."

Arowan watched as the other men, gently at first, got Mouse to defend herself with the sticks and rocks and then attack with the knife. They spread out and came at her from the front and from behind. She held the stick firmly and confidently, the strength in her arms surprised Arowan. The men weren't using their full strength but they were certainly putting her through her paces. At one point one of the men came at her from behind and Mouse swivelled round so quickly that she caught him with her outstretched arm and knocked him off balance, narrowly missing him with her knife. As he regained his composure, the group laughed at the fact that this rather large man had been knocked down by a twelve year old girl.

"You're a fast learner young lady." Said Arowan, who knew she must have listened to every word he had said when he was showing her some moves, and apart from someone with a little wounded pride, he knew that all of them were impressed by her.

However, they also all knew that doing it 'for real' would

be different matter entirely.

"Well done Mouse." Said Arowan.

"Remind me not to get into a fight with you!" Laughed Angel, "you were quite scary when you attacked with a knife."

"I've used one before remember." Mouse smiled weakly.

"Ok, let's sit and get our breath back and go over Inanya's route." Said Arowan patting a large rock next to him, indicating that they should all sit for a while.

"I know it off by heart," said Mouse, "I've been going over it again and again in my head."

"Good girl."

And Mouse then surprised them all, yet again by saying "If it's ok, I'd just like to get on with it?"

Arowan looked at Angel and their five companions, and couldn't think of a single excuse, apart from the obvious dangers, for her not to go.

"Ok, well, if you're sure you're ready." He said.

"Come here Mouse." Said Angel. The two girls hugged and Angel wished her good luck and quickly ran back to the river, dove straight in and was swimming at considerable speed in no time.

"She's not good with goodbyes," explained Arowan, "not since her mother..."

"It's ok Arowan," replied Mouse, "I understand."

"Yes, good." He shuffled about a bit and it was then that Mouse realised Angel wasn't the only one who struggled with goodbyes. Mouse touched his arm and just said "I'm ready."

"Are you sure you don't want to go through what's in your bag one last time?"

"It's ok Arowan, I've been sat here with my hand in the

bag feeling what's in there, getting used to the feel of all the different objects."

"A true hunter." Announced Arowan proudly.

There was another awkward shuffle of feet and a momentary silence before Arowan ushered them back towards the river.

Just as they jumped into the water, unexpectedly the heavens opened and a wind, so strong, gusted through the island. Six white heads and a dark blonde head surfaced and were instantly battered by the rain.

Mouse looked at Arowan, who looked positively puzzled.

"I don't know why," she shouted above the noise of the heavy rain and howling wind, "but I never expected it to rain here!"

"To be honest Mouse, we don't ever get this sort of weather!" He yelled back.

The seven of them just bobbed up and down for a while to see if the unusual storm would pass.

It didn't.

"We might as well swim up river to the tunnel and shelter for a bit?" Suggested Arowan.

Everyone nodded, they weren't getting anywhere by just 'staying put'.

"But Arowan," said Mouse, "what about the Verzillas?"

"We'll be ok while it's raining Mouse, they don't like water of any kind so they'll have retreated back into their caves for now."

Relief washed over Mouse, just as the rain was doing.

"Ok, let's go!" She yelled.

The swim up river was not as easy as yesterday, the torrential rain was unforgiving and the wind just seemed to keep pushing them back to where they had started. But they battled on and eventually managed to find the spot where they had leapt into the water, only yesterday, and survived the attack of the Verzilla.

Wearily they heaved their tired, sodden bodies out of the river and onto the bank. They stayed close to the water for a while, to catch their breath in relative safety.

Arowan looked at his five friends, "Can you believe this?" He said, "I've never known weather like it."

They all commented on the freak weather and all looked at Mouse. She was a bedraggled sight; wet hair plastered to her face, wide, searching eyes, mouth turned down in concentration and all of this huddled into a shivering little ball on the edge of the riverbank.

"I think we should get going Mouse." Arowan said.

"Yes, ok."

"It'll be much safer for you while it's raining, you know, to make your way through the jungle and up the volcano."

"Ok. I'm ready for the next bit." And with that she took a deep breath, stood up, stretched and made sure her bag was still secure around her waist.

With everyone ready, they tentatively made their way towards the unfamiliar tunnel. Three of the men went in front, Arowan by Mouse's side and two of the men bringing up the rear.

Up ahead the large tropical jungle trees were swaying violently in the wind whilst the noise of the rain, as it hit the enormous leaves, echoed around the island.

Mouse was far from comforted by the weather.

Regardless of the wind and rain they reached the path that lead to the tunnel. Gingerly they all walked the few metres along the path and stopped in front of the entrance.

The tunnel had filled with water a bit more from all the

rain but was still easily accessible.

"We'll come through the tunnel with you Mouse and assess the situation at the other end."

"Ok, let's go then."

They stayed in the same formation as they walked down into the gloom of the tunnel. It was very similar to the Bichir tunnel; it was cold, wet and very dark.

The seven of them linked hands as they waded through the waist high water, and slowly inched forward into the darkness. The tunnel was quite a bit longer than 'their' tunnel but eventually they could see the dim daylight at the other end, and could still hear the rain lashing down.

Carefully the first three men exited the tunnel, had a quick look around the surrounding area, and then motioned the others to follow.

As they came out of the tunnel they found themselves deep in the heart of the jungle; thick with trees of all sizes, waist high undergrowth in some places, and very humid, heavy air.

As they all gazed about they noticed that there were very definite paths trodden through the grasses and bushes and although none of them wanted to think about what had made the paths, Mouse could at least find a way through the jungle.

"Ok Mouse, although it's still raining, we really can't go any further." Said Arowan.

"It's ok, I'll be fine." Her shaky voice gave her away and Arowan's heart tightened.

"We just can't risk it drying up and us being too far away from the water."

"I know where I have to go."

"We'll be waiting the other side of the tunnel in a few

hours time. Just give us a shout when you are back and we'll come through and get you."

And although she hadn't had much conversation with the five men, there were hugs and words of support from all of them.

Arowan turned to her last of all, placed his long hands on her shoulders and smiled.

"You are a very brave young lady, and hopefully all of this will be over soon. The Trident will grant Inanya peace at last and it will get you back to your family."

"Let's hope so."

"Be careful Mouse and come back to us safely." He plopped a kiss on top of her head and pulled her into a watery embrace.

He pulled away after a moment and tucked a bit of wet hair behind her ear and turned towards the tunnel where the others were waiting.

Mouse stood and watched them leave.

She felt very alone and very scared.

*

Inanya's tail was whipping to and fro in the dark gloomy water. She hadn't been able to relax ever since she'd left Arowan and the girl yesterday. She couldn't believe that after all this time she would finally be free of this imprisoned lifestyle. She would be able to swim to the surface, feel the warm sun on her face, she would be beautiful, like all those other willowy mer-maids, and live the rest of her life in happiness.

As the last one of her kind, all the other tortured ancestors now gone, she would bring the curse full circle and finish her life as her family had started theirs all those hundreds of years ago ... as mer-people.

*

'Ok Mouse, come on, this is getting you nowhere' she thought as she still stood rooted to the spot, minutes later.
But all the while it was raining she felt a little, and just a little, bit safer. The rain wasn't beating down on her face as it had been earlier but it was still raining and the wind was still blowing the foliage around her.
"Right, I need to head East, which must mean I go right." She muttered to herself.
Thankfully there was a pathway through the jungle which headed East.
She took one cautious step forward, then another, then another.
She was on her way to retrieve the lost Trident and change people's lives forever.

*

Something stirred him from unconsciousness.
It was someone coming.
Help at last.
He tried to shout out – nothing would come.
He tried to open his eyes but only one eye half opened to reveal a small slit of light, blurry and dull.
Then he saw her.
That girl!
She was the cause of all of this. All he wanted was for the Serpent Queen to get her back to her world so he and

Angel could be best friends again.

He missed Angel.

He hated Mouse.

But she might be the only one who could get him back to Bichir. Back to Angel.

He tried to move but he couldn't feel his limbs, he couldn't lift his head.

It was hopeless.

She was gone.

*

With the rain still pounding at the trees around her Mouse was unable to listen out for any unwelcome surprises. Visibility was also tricky as everything from ground level upwards was moving with each gust of wind.

Each step was tentative and slow, but Mouse willed herself forward. Through the swaying trees and the rustling foliage she went until she came to an area where, if the sun could have, it would have shone through to the clear patch of long grasses in the small clearing. There were flowers of all sizes and colours dotted about which was a brief reprise from the cloying green of the jungle which seemed to consume her. The flowers were dancing in the wind but remained rooted to the spot at the same time.

Mouse took in the rest of the clearing and noticed that the path seemed to go in different directions but there was still a path which headed East.

As she looked up, through the rain, she got the first glimpse of the volcano she was about to climb. It was on her left as she looked at it, which meant she was at least going the right way. The base of the volcano at this point was just a sheer cliff and as her eyes followed it upwards she could just make out the three peaks that were once under water, many years ago. A lot had changed since then.

And so, with a determined stride, she carried on, desperate to get this over with as soon as possible.

The trodden down path headed back into the density of the jungle but stayed close enough to the base of the volcano for Mouse to know she was still on track.

After several minutes, and no surprises, she came to a large stretch of land with boulders scattered amongst the grass.

The grave site.

Thankfully it wasn't like the graveyard that Mouse had pictured in her head. It wasn't scary at all, and apart from the sound of the rain and the wind, the area was somehow peaceful.

The boulders themselves didn't resemble shells much anymore, just lumps of rock which were now covered in moss and surrounded by billowy grass.

"So ... the path in the rock face," she mumbled to herself, "gotta be here somewhere."

She let her hands trail over the tops of the boulders as she approached the volcano. The base wasn't as clear to see at this point, as there were shrubs and small trees growing around the bottom and up the much more gentle slopes.

With the rain and wind easing slightly Mouse got to work straight away; pulling shrubs aside, using her knife to cut the thicker vegetation and wading through the long grass to look for the path carved into the rock.

She was about to give up as her hands hurt, she had scratches on her legs and she couldn't see any sign of a path!

It wasn't until she stopped, sighed, and stepped back to look up at the volcano that she saw a path etched into the rock above the tops of the trees! She followed the zigzag downwards until it disappeared into the trees. She took a guess at where it might have ended up, should she have been able to see it all the way down to the ground, and marched off in that direction to find it. It took a while but then, there, behind a large tree was the path.

It wasn't covered with plants, nor was it unclear. If she had carried on looking, she would have come across it eventually. Before beginning her ascent she noticed that there was a different type of tree growing in patches above the pathway, they looked older and gnarled, bent over and almost dead looking, with some branches striking downwards into the path and trying to block the way. A complete contrast to the lush green trees of the jungle. She also noticed that the stone slabs Inanya had mentioned were all but gone, just a few remained at the bottom of the path but then there was just rubble.

Mouse kept her knife in her hand and ventured forth, she decided there was no point in standing still just looking at the volcano.

It was quite a steep slope, which wouldn't have mattered to the mer-people as they swam along it all those years ago, but walking up it was strenuous to say the least.

Although it was slow going, soon Mouse was above the trees and was able to see the magnificent view which lay before her. The huge expanse of green jungle at her feet was breathtaking and then beyond that, the cool aqua coloured ocean, still sparkling and defying the dark morbid skies.

Finally she tore her eyes away from the sea and searched

for Bichir. She spotted a rocky rise in the landscape and a sparseness of jungle vegetation, she surmised that she had found it.

She thought of the villagers and how they would all be thinking about her.

She thought about Tang and how his disappearance had affected them all.

And she thought about Angel, and about how much she'd hated being left out of this particular adventure. Mouse smiled.

She looked up ahead, along the path, and decided it was time to carry on.

She continued up the path, more slowly now as the rain had practically stopped and an eerie silence had settled over the island. All that could be heard was the occasional 'plop' as the rainwater fell from leaf to leaf until it eventually found the ground.

Mouse estimated that she must be over halfway and assumed she would see the Cave of Thrones very soon.

Taking steady breaths she continued upwards.

BANG!

The thunderous sound startled Mouse and she fell to the ground.

The ground which was now shaking.

CRACK!

The rock around the path was virtually splitting in two!

Mouse eased her way to the side of the path as small stones and rubble spilt down the side of the volcano. She tried to hide herself, to avoid being struck by falling debris, under one of the old trees that grew on the edge of the pathway.

BANG!

The tree above her shook and more rocks hailed down

above her and hit the tree's branches with force.

Mouse tried to curl herself into a small ball under the protection of the tree whilst the earthquake persisted, and the ground continued to shudder.

The path now had a crack running down the middle of it but at the moment it wasn't damaging enough for her not to be able to continue.

If the earthquake stopped.

Then it got much worse for Mouse.

A huge boulder from higher up, hurtled down the side of the volcano and hit the tree that Mouse was cowered under.

The trunk of the tree immediately broke off and sent it crashing down on top of Mouse!

She screamed as the branches struck her and landed across the pathway. Luckily the width of the path stopped the tree from fully falling as it wedged itself across the gap. The branches which had pinned Mouse down were thankfully only thin ones.

All except one.

Mouse had a few scratches from the spindly branches as they had unexpectedly fallen on top of her but one very thick, heavy branch had landed on her foot.

Mouse fought back the tears that were threatening to spill down her face as the rumbling ceased and an almost spiritual silence ensued.

She leant forward to see if she could push the branch away from her foot. The branch had snapped free from the rest of the tree when it had landed with a crashing thump, onto the path and Mouse's foot.

Thankfully Mouse could still wiggle her toes and could see that the full weight of the branch was being supported by a new pile of rocks which had formed in the last few minutes. If that pile had not been there, she knew her ankle would have been snapped in two. The good news was that she could feel all the movement in her foot, the bad news was that she could not shift the branch.

"Oh brilliant!" She hissed to herself, and brushed the leaves and snapped smaller branches away from her face.

SNAP!

Mouse stopped what she was doing, absolutely certain that it wasn't her that made that last noise. With searching eyes she tried to see through the branches of the fallen tree and along the path. At first she couldn't see anything but tree and rock but then she saw something that practically stopped her heart.

A pair of hungry, beady, black eyes staring straight at her!

"Oh noooo!" She whispered, and then held her breath.

The Verzilla had definitely seen her before she had seen it. She was forced to remain where she was and any futile attempts to free herself were long gone.

Only then did a single tear roll down her cheek.

She looked at the beast, straight in the eyes. It hadn't moved ... yet.

She heard another sound of movement from behind the Verzilla.

"Please no, not more of them." She whimpered.

Petrified, she could only watch as another pair of beady dark eyes found her, and stared.

The next thing she knew, the loudest crunching and crashing of jaws ricocheted along the path, through the fallen tree and was booming into her ears.

The two Verzillas were literally chewing their way through the branches and getting closer to where Mouse was trapped.

An involuntary scream escaped from her mouth as she tried to back further into the solid rock wall, and although she gritted her teeth through the pain of trying to pull her foot away from the branch, she couldn't get away from the two snarling beasts which were nearly upon her.

The noise was terrifying as they crashed through the branches towards her; pounding feet supporting enormous bodies, crunching jaws dripping with drool, and snarls and growls of excitement as their prey was only feet away.

The Verzillas were side by side, working as a team to get to Mouse through the fallen tree, and although she wanted to close her eyes, she couldn't help looking from one to the other.

She looked at the beast who had arrived second and all of a sudden it stopped in its tracks.

Recognition dawned.

On both parts.

He was close enough now for Mouse to see the healed wound above his leg.

She was close enough now for the Verzilla to realise that this was the girl who had prompted the others to save his life.

The first Verzilla paused for the briefest moment then carried on chomping at the last few twig like branches which separated it from Mouse.

She could smell it's breath, she could see the steam coming off it's hot, wet, scaly body, she held out her knife in a shaky hand.

Mouse wouldn't ever have guessed at what happened next.

The first Verzilla was one bite away from getting its first

taste of pure human, when the second Verzilla lunged forward, scaring the life out of Mouse as he was practically on top of her, and stopped it in its tracks.

There was some low growling noises from both beasts as they squared up to each other. One (hopefully) protecting her and one trying to eat her.

'Surreal' thought Mouse.

Abruptly the growling noises stopped, quickly followed by gnashing of teeth as the two creatures went for one another.

Luckily for Mouse the second Verzilla had a slight size advantage and managed to push the other backwards a little way. He seized the opportunity to take a few large steps back, avoiding treading on Mouse, and then charged forwards and smashed into the other somewhat shocked predator! It careened into the path wall with a pitiful yelp and struggled to its feet.

The stronger of the two stood his ground and thumped his big feet on the rubble and broken tree as a warning to back off.

For a moment Mouse thought it was going to return the charge and then both huge beasts would end up on top of her!

But the first Verzilla obviously knew when it was beaten and so it raised up on it's back legs, dropped to the ground with a thud, roared and backed away.

There was then a moment of slight deliberation for Mouse. Did this Verzilla want to protect her or did this Verzilla want to eat her for himself?

As he turned towards her, with his mouth wide open, she all of a sudden doubted he was protecting her!

He moved towards her, slowly and deliberately.

With her hand still half outstretched and clutching the small knife, she realised that she had no real defence against these hideous, almost prehistoric creatures.

She lowered her arm and put the knife on the ground, beaten.

The Verzilla watched her.

CRACK!

The heavy branch which lay across her foot had just been bitten in half and it now lay amongst the other shreds of tree which lay scattered across the path.

Mouse slowly pulled her foot free and although it was hurting a bit, it wasn't broken and she would be able to continue.

She and the Verzilla looked at each other for a few silent moments, with understanding.

And as Mouse gently rubbed her throbbing foot, the Verzilla turned and walked back down the path, the way it had come.

Mouse picked up the knife and stood up slowly, testing her foot. It was ok, it would be a little bruised but the swimming would do it good when she got back to Bichir.

She stepped over the debris which, only minutes before, had been a healthy living tree, and looked upwards towards the top of the volcano which was now bathed in warm sunshine.

With a deep breath and not allowing herself to dwell on what had just happened, she carried on up the zigzagging path, cautiously peering round corners as she went, until she reached an area where the path widened in front of an opening in the sheer rock face.

Whether or not the 'opening' was in fact a cave, needed further investigation, but there were also a few crumbling boulders in front of the prospective cave which could have been the king's throne at one time, in the very distant past. A throne where a king had sat and addressed his people.

With a quick look around the area and seeing nothing alarming, Mouse moved towards the rock face.

She realised it was definitely big enough to be *the* cave when she pulled back the hanging vine like leaves from the entrance and could see the size of the opening.

Caves didn't hold the same fear for Mouse as they had done only months before. Having been abducted from one, by a half dragon/half human, and living to tell the tale, she'd got used to the dark wet gloom that presented itself now.

The cave looked empty, probably ransacked by various creatures over the centuries, and no longer held the treasures of a royal family.

The further she ventured, the darker it got and the less she could see. But she thought she spotted an even darker area towards the back wall of the cave which may lead to another inner chamber.

Inanya, for all her faults, had been right so far.

Mouse made her way to the second chamber but it was too dark to see anything at all. So remembering back to her previous cave exploits she realised she needed to make a torch of some description.

She stumbled back out into the brilliant sunshine which initially dazzled her, but after a few 'blinks' she was scrabbling about trying to find relatively dry sticks to tie together and set on fire to use as a makeshift torch.

The vine leaves were perfect for tying up the sticks, and using her knife she secured the funny looking bouquet together.

Now to start a fire.

She had heard that you need to rub sticks together, but she wasn't sure if that was what her mum called 'an old wives tale' and didn't really work at all.

She didn't have any other options so she started to rub two smaller, drier twigs together.

After what seemed like an age, with the sun beating down, she finally got a small wisp of smoke and then a tiny flame.

She lowered the precious little flame onto her pile of sticks. It didn't 'take' immediately as some of the sticks were slightly damp from the downpour but with patience and a lot of whispered 'pleases', the torch was finally glowing.

Proudly Mouse entered the cave once more.

It seemed bigger now she could see it all but still just as empty.

She approached the second chamber, her torch held out in front of her, and squeezed through the small gap.

What she saw before her took her breath away! The whole area sparkled in a million different lights, in every colour, shapes and sizes imaginable.

"Wow!" Gushed Mouse as she stood transfixed. Her eyes scanned the piles of jewellery, piles of bowls and dishes, and amongst the glittery piles were several bejewelled crowns!

What she couldn't see was anything that resembled a trident.

She stepped into the chamber a bit further, careful not to touch anything, and peered around the corner of what now appeared to be an 'L' shaped space.

And there, casually tossed in the very far corner was, what looked to her, like a trident.

Not a magical looking trident by any means, just a rotting,

wooden handled fork with a few lacklustre gems in the prongs.

Mouse looked around at the piles of jewels and decided she'd better search around amongst it all to find the trident everyone was expecting her to bring back.

So, propping her torch in one of the piles, she started to scrummidge amongst the treasures.

She found nothing that even looked right.

She glanced back at the old, long handled fork in the corner on its own. That had to be it, although she wasn't 100% certain that Inanya would agree.

"Oh well," she sighed with resignation, "you're coming with me."

She bent down to pick up the fork and the very second she touched the near crumbled handle a brilliant light blinded her!

FLASH – her house.

FLASH – her mum and dad.

FLASH – her school.

FLASH – the willow tree.

Visions flashed before her eyes and when she could see properly again, she looked down at the once rotten old fork to see now, a beautiful, shiny, bejewelled trident! She blinked a few times but what she saw was definitely different from what she had discovered in the cave, cast aside as if worthless.

The Lost Trident.

***

Chapter Ten

Mouse gazed at the newly transformed Trident in her hand, and knew instantly that this would be her way home. She looked around at all the other glistening treasures knowing they needed to remain where they were. The people of Bichir had no need for riches. So she picked up the torch in the other hand, went back through to the main cave and then out into the sunshine.

She snuffed out the torch using a large wet leaf and started to head back down the zigzaggy path.

It somehow felt steeper going downwards but her injured foot obviously didn't help. She was wary of going too fast because her ankle was still quite swollen, but excitement and hope propelled her down to the bottom in no time, without any further sightings of drooling, hungry beasts.

Mouse retraced her steps through the jungle and back towards the tunnel where she would call for Arowan and no longer be alone.

The trek seemed longer on the way back and Mouse was beginning to think she had taken the wrong path when she had got to the stone shells, as there had been several to chose from. However she was sure she was right so continued on the same route and eventually she could see the tunnel. Mouse never thought she'd ever been happier to see a dark, wet hole in the ground!

She was nearly at the mouth of the tunnel and not really concentrating, when she caught her foot on some vegetation and she stumbled to the ground. She looked back to see where her foot was snagged and immediately let out an ear piercing scream!

It wasn't a branch which had trapped her foot at all.

A bloodied hand was gripped tightly around her ankle and not letting go!

Mouse screamed again.

She daren't move – she couldn't move.

Relief washed over her as soon as she heard Arowan's echoey shouting as he and the five men sploshed through the tunnel. They seemed to take forever to get to her, and once through, Arowan rushed to her side instantly.

"What is it Mouse, are you hurt?"

Unable to speak, she just pointed to her foot.

Arowan followed her pointed finger and gasped as he saw why she had screamed.

He leapt to his feet and looked down at the hand, the webbed hand, currently attached to Mouse's foot.

"Tang!" He exclaimed.

The others had now joined them and everyone seemed to panic at once. Arowan could see that Mouse hadn't come back from the trek unscathed as her face, arms and legs were covered in scratches, and he could also see The

Trident laid down on the grass beside her.

"Mouse, are you ok for a moment whilst I see to Tang?" He asked.

"Of course Arowan, I didn't mean to alarm anyone but it was a bit of a shock seeing his hand on my ankle all of a sudden!"

"And your ankle, it's ok, it looks quite swollen?"

"It's ok, bit painful, but ok."

Arowan gently stroked Mouse's cheek and smiled, "You are an exceptional girl."

Mouse watched as the six men had to prize Tang's rigid hand from her foot and then gently move him out of the soft, muddy ditch where he had been for the last few days. He was not conscious, he was broken, and he was barely breathing. Mouse saw that his body was covered in blood and his fin was torn and colourless, as the men carefully carried him towards the tunnel, towards Bichir.

Mouse stood up, picked up The Trident and followed.

"Mouse," said Arowan, "are you ok on your own or do you need help?"

"I'm ok thanks, I'll just follow you guys."

"Your ankle?"

"It's ok, I'll tell you all about it when we get back."

"Ok, if you're sure."

"I am, let's get going."

It wasn't easy carrying a motionless Tang through the narrow tunnel but slowly and carefully they got to the other end and back to more familiar territory.

Tang still hadn't moved or opened his eyes.

"It's not going to be easy, swimming in the river and trying to keep him flat." Said one of the men.

"We'll have to try to keep near to the bank where it's

hopefully shallower, so we can carry on walking with him." Replied Arowan.

"Shall I swim ahead and get help?" Suggested Mouse.

"Good idea Mouse," said Arowan, "you know you're way back ok?"

"Yep!" And with that she hobbled up to the edge of the river, dove in and swam back to the Bichir tunnel. None of which was easy with a massive fork in tow.

She emerged from the tunnel onto the beach area and must've looked quite a sight because within seconds she was surrounded and carried back to a sandy spot on the beach, with water and food thrust at her from all directions.

Angel was by her side instantly and nearly squeezed the life out of her.

"You made it." She sighed and noticed tears in her friend's eyes.

"I did, but I won't be able to breathe for much longer if you don't let go!" Mouse laughed.

Angel sprung back, "Oh, I'm sorry Mouse, are you hurt?"

"Just a sore ankle."

"Thank goodness. And you got The Trident. I knew you would."

"I nearly didn't but I'll tell you about that later but I have to get help for Arowan and the others."

"Why do they need help? Where are they?"

"Angel, calm down. We found Tang." All of a sudden the beach area went quiet, "They need help carrying him back, he's in a really bad way."

She didn't have to say it twice, half the villagers shot through the tunnel immediately.

Mouse finally let the emotions of the last few hours catch

up with her. She could see that Angel was torn between sitting with her and going to see Tang, but she really couldn't stop the tears that flowed freely down her face. Realisation that she was nearly killed, again, was finally hitting home, with such force that she couldn't help herself.

Angel stayed with her and hugged her while she sobbed and until the villagers finally brought Tang back through the tunnel.

Angel leapt to her feet and rushed over to the group of men carrying him, "Tang!" She cried.

"He can't hear you Angel," said Arowan, "he's in a very critical condition."

"What can we do dad?"

"First we need to get him in the water, see if we can hydrate him and wash all this dried blood away."

Arowan and the villagers gently carried him across the beach and laid him down in the shallow water. His mum and dad held him with tears running down their cheeks; they had Tang back but no one knew if he would survive whatever ordeal he'd been through. They washed all the blood off his face and body only to reveal massive bruising which covered most of him from head to toe!

"Oh Tang." His mum wept openly.

The next few hours were spent getting Tang hydrated, clean and comfortable, and getting Mouse calmed down after her trek, of which no one knew anything about yet. While Tang was being cared for, Mouse sat on the water's edge and swished her foot about in the cool refreshing water which helped the swelling. She then went for a quiet swim to clean her own cuts and scrapes, the villagers allowing her time to be on her own.

Mouse watched as Tang was eventually taken out of the water, still unconscious, wrapped in one of the wet blankets used at night time, and he was taken to Arowan's dwelling as it was near to the water and near to where everyone sat. His mum stayed with him the whole time.

Finally everyone was sat down, food was being prepared and all were eagerly waiting to hear about how Mouse got The Trident.

Arowan addressed his fellow villagers:

"Well, it's been quite a day for all of us one way or another but before we hear about Mouse and her incredible trek this morning I just want to update you on Tang's health. He is still unconscious so we have no idea how on earth he ended up in such a bad way but thankfully whoever did this to him, left him near water. If he hadn't been in the ditch where it was all damp and wet he would definitely not be alive, and obviously our unusual outburst of weather helped too. However, the fact that he's 'hung in there' for all this time is a good sign and although not out of the woods, his skin reacted well to the soaking in the pool and we'll all keep an eye on him at all times."

He watched them all digest the severity of Tang's condition and let them discuss the situation.

When eventually the chatter ceased, he continued.

"So, the other news of the day – well, the century actually – is how Mouse managed to get hold of The Trident. I think we'd all like to congratulate her on being so brave, being all alone in a place she barely knows and amazingly finding and retrieving The Trident, and bringing it back to us."

There was clapping and cheering and Mouse could feel the admiration and respect envelope her.

She stood up and held The Trident next to her.

"So Mouse, do you want to tell us what happened to you today?" Asked Arowan.

Mouse giggled, "I think I've just about got over the shock, enough to tell the story."

So she started at the beginning, from when Arowan and his friends left her, and told them step by step exactly what happened.

The million questions which followed were mainly about two parts of the story: One, the amazement at the Verzillas reaction to her, and two, what happened when she first touched The Trident.

"Ok, ok everyone!" Yelled Arowan, over the various conversations, "I think we'll all agree that we are very lucky to have Mouse back with us. And thankfully we now know that The Trident still holds magical powers after all this time."

All the white heads bobbed up and down as they nodded in agreement.

"Are we really going to hand it back to Inanya tomorrow?" Asked Angel.

"We promised we would, so we will. Then after she has done with it, we will bring Mouse back here to get her normal clothes and shoes, find the willow tree and get her home."

Angel looked at Mouse, "It'll be weird without you here now." She said sadly.

"I know, this feels like a second home to me. Just like the dragon's world did."

"Do you still remember them all?"

"Every one of them, and I have my beautiful little red crystal to remind me."

"I hope you remember us, coz I doubt anyone will ever forget you."

The two girls hugged and wandered back to Angel's dwelling where they settled down for the night, after what seemed like a very long day. They chatted lazily about the memories Mouse would take back with her, whilst the villagers remained on the beach discussing The Trident and the possibilities tomorrow could bring.

*

"How did you sleep Mouse?" Asked Arowan as the girls got to the beach the next morning.

"Very well thanks Arowan, I was pooped!"

Arowan put his arm around the two girls and lead them to a spot on the beach next to Bangus and Trahira.

"Will you come for a swim with us?" Asked Bangus.

"Of course, come on." Angel, Mouse, Bangus and Trahira ran from the beach into the shallow waters, and splashed their way into the pool. The sun was shining brightly through the hole in the ceiling of Bichir, heating up the lagoon to tropical temperatures, so when their warm bodies hit the cool water there were shrieks of shock and surprise echoing around the stone walls.

Angel and Mouse splashed about with the little ones for a while, throwing them high into the air and watching them splosh back into the water with squeals of delight, then hiding underwater and coming up to the surface when they least expected it. Before long Bangus and Trahira got bored and went off to find their own friends. Angel and Mouse were soon joined by Bonito, Vimba and Mora.

"Have you seen Tang this morning?" Vimba asked Angel.

"Not yet, but word is that he's still the same, you know, not awake, but his breathing is better."

"I'm sure he'll be ok." Said Bonito.

Angel smiled and hoped, with all her heart, that he was right.

The friends all completed a few full circuits of the pool and were just wading through the shallow water when Tang's mum lead a group of villagers, carrying Tang, down to the water. As they passed by, the five friends they all noticed how much more colour he had in his face.

The slow moving group gently laid Tang into the water and Tang's mum used her hands to swoosh the cool, refreshing water over her son, his limp body still unresponsive. The next few day's care of Tang would be crucial, if in fact, he pulled through.

As they all wandered up onto the beach Arowan approached them and smiled.

"So Mouse, are you ready to see Inanya and hand over The Trident?"

"I s'pose so." Mouse replied but Arowan wasn't convinced.

"It'll be ok, and once she's done with it, we'll say our goodbyes and get you back home."

"Can't you stay a bit longer Mouse?" Pleaded Angel.

"I suppose one more day can't hurt?" Replied Mouse. They both looked at Arowan with big sad eyes and hopeful faces.

"We'll see," he replied, "it depends on how things go with Inanya first."

The girls looked at each other knowing full well they would win him round and be able to spend one more day together. A day of messing about with the others in the sea, with Torpedo and Discus. Some time spent lounging about in Bichir. A proper day to prepare to say good bye.

"When are we going Arowan?" Asked Mouse.

"To see Inanya?"

"Yes. I'm ready."

"We'll leave in a minute, I just need to make sure Bangus and Trahira are being watched while we are away from Bichir, then we'll go."

"We'll go and get a supply of Oxystemla." Said Angel.

So Angel and Mouse scampered off to get themselves all ready to go whilst Arowan checked that his other two children would be ok, rounded up his friends, grabbed some weapons and The Trident.

Within half an hour the men were assembled on the beach with the necessary precautionary weapons and The Trident but were still waiting for Angel and Mouse. Eventually they sauntered over and joined Arowan and his friends.

Before they departed they all stood still and watched Tang being carried back up to Arowan's dwelling, still unconscious and now wrapped in a wet blanket, and no change to his condition.

The villagers of Bichir struggled with their emotions as they watched Tang and his family trying to be positive, and they watched Arowan prepare his little party for the unknown ... once again.

Everything stopped when a shout from inside Arowan's dwelling echoed around Bichir!

"Tang!" Called his mum.

Arowan sped into his dwelling.

"What is it?"

"He ... he ... he opened his eyes!"

196

All the villagers crowded around the small entrance and tried to hear and see what was going on. Angel pushed her way through the crowd and rushed to where Tang lay, on Arowan's rocky bed.

"Tang, it's Angel." She cried, tears welling up in her big sad eyes.

Tang's mum stroked his long white hair.

"Tang, Angel's here." She said.

They all watched as his eyes flickered open and closed. Opened and closed.

"A-A-Angel." He whispered, so quietly it was barely audible.

"Tang, it's me, I'm here. You're home safe."

Tears of relief and joy poured from the eyes of all who could hear and see them. There wasn't a dry eye in the whole of Bichir.

Tang's eyes were barely open but as they settled on Angel, the corners of his mouth turned upwards ever so slightly.

Angel leaned in so he could see she was still there and she thought she heard him try to say something else. It sounded like "Inanya" but the sound was so quiet she couldn't be sure.

"Sssshhh," she said, "just rest and get better, we'll talk when you're stronger."

"Ok everyone," said Arowan, "let's give him some space and let him rest."

He ushered all the villagers back onto the beach and away from his dwelling, and left Tang with his family in peace and quiet.

Mouse gave Angel a hug and said "I'm glad he's going to be ok."

"Let's hope so, then we can find out what happened to

him."

Arowan interrupted them and asked if they were ready.

So, once again Arowan, his four friends, Angel and Mouse prepared to go and meet Inanya.

The wishes of good luck were louder and happier now that Tang had woken up, and an infectious air of positivity spread through Bichir.

So as the seven of them sploshed through the tunnel, The Trident securely strapped to Arowan's side, they were filled with hope for whatever may happen in the next few hours.

They emerged through the tunnel into the river and the sun shone down on them as if to emphasise their mood. They got to 'the rock' and ate some Oxystemla, then swam down river and into the sea.

They were joined by Torpedo and Discus who couldn't understand why no one had been to play with them recently and why no one seemed to want to play today either. It seemed that no amount of nudging or tricks could entice anyone to join in. They soon gave up and were content to trail behind the preoccupied group as they headed towards the meeting place, in deeper waters.

As they swam deeper, the water cooled their skin and got darker and murkier, and before long they reached the rocky seabed where Inanya was already waiting.

They all watched her dark eyes light up when she saw what was strapped to Arowan's side.

"The Trident!" She screeched, "You got it!"

As they got closer Arowan gripped the prized possession tightly, he was not prepared to just hand it over as soon as they got there. He needed some reassurances first. He needed to know that Inanya would be handing The Trident back after she had finished with it.

Arms outstretched, the Serpent Queen approached them.

"It's beautiful," she said, "give it to me,"

"Not so fast," said Arowan as he held The Trident behind his back, "I need to know what happens after you're done with it."

Aghast at the gall of Arowan, she scowled at him and replied "Once I am transformed back into a proper mermaid, Arowan, you can do whatever you like with it."

The serpents, who seemed to appear from nowhere, started furious circling movements around Inanya, hissing and snarling at her.

Inanya realised her mistake.

"I meant," she stuttered, "once me *and* my serpents have been transformed."

The writhing mass of appeased serpents slowed and they moved behind her.

Angel and Mouse, in their protective circle, quite happily just peeped out from behind the large bodies of Arowan and his four friends.

"Ok." Said Arowan.

He moved towards her and held The Trident in front of him for Inanya to take.

Suddenly nervous, Inanya swam towards him.

She hesitated as she moved to take The Trident but eventually, finally, had it in her grasp.

There was a loud crackle and a flash of brilliant light as her hand touched it for the first time.

Arowan shot backwards to his wary group and they all watched as Inanya's dark face lit up, her eyes hungry and greedy, as more crackles and flashes followed.

It was like watching a rapid underwater thunderstorm!

Inanya stretched her long sleek body fully, held The Trident out in front of her as she waited for the transformation to take place.

Angel and Mouse stared with open mouths and clung to Arowan as their circle formed a line to view the spectacle before them.

They also watched as the flashes dimmed, the crackles stopped and Inanya could still be known as the Serpent Queen.

There had been no transformation!

Inanya's face changed from triumph, to confusion, to fury in the space of a minute.

The Trident fell from her hand and dropped to the seabed.

Angel and Mouse returned to their position behind Arowan and they suspected that the long ear piercing scream would have been heard throughout all the oceans in the world!

Inanya's whole body was shaking with anger and her eyes were as black as coal as she searched for Mouse in the gloomy water.

"WHAT. DID. YOU. DO. TO. IT?" She spat.

Arowan held Mouse firmly behind him. "She did nothing Inanya, she went and got it, just as you asked. She nearly got killed in the process!"

"SO. WHY. DIDN'T. IT. WORK?" Inanya hissed as she slowly inched towards them with wild hair and whipping tail.

"I don't know Inanya." Replied Arowan moving his group backwards, away from her.

There was another long shriek as she began to swim furiously round and round in a circle.

The serpents joined in and the water around them soon

formed an underwater whirlpool. The force of which began to suck in small fish and anything else which happened to float by.

Round and round they swam, the serpents and Inanya.

Angel and Mouse screamed as they could all feel the almost magnetic pull of the Serpent Queen and the serpents as they got faster and faster and the whirlpool got stronger and stronger.

The turbulent water was already lifting small rocks off the bottom of the seabed and hurling them upwards into the dangerous spiral.

Arowan, his friends, Angel and Mouse couldn't fight the strength of the swirling water and got sucked in closer and closer.

Arowan desperately tried to force Angel and Mouse away from the spiral but couldn't compete with the sheer power of the raging snare.

One by one they were yanked into the vortex and separated from each other. A muddle of arms, tails and legs appeared at random intervals as the bodies slowly spun upwards.

Arowan would never quite comprehend how Inanya managed it, but the Serpent Queen sought out Mouse, focussed her enraged energy on getting close to her and with a massive surge forward, grabbed her by the hair.

She tugged at the frightened girl until their faces were inches apart.

"You did this and you will PAY!" She yelled.

Arowan used all his strength to try and get to Mouse and as long as he lived would not forget the look on Mouse's face as the Serpent Queen held her outside the spiral, still by her hair, and with a long vicious flick of her tail, catapulted her at great speed into a large boulder!

Mouse hit the rock full force with her head, and then gently drifted down to the seabed, leaving a thin trail of bright red blood behind her.

Arowan lunged at Inanya and put his hands around her throat, causing the whirlpool to falter and bodies crash into each other.

The force of the water was still whipping them all in a circular motion but one by one they were all able to escape its grasp.

The serpents battled against the confused current towards Inanya while Angel swam to Mouse. Arowan swatted two evil serpents away with his long, strong arm as they tried to free Inanya from his clutches but more kept coming!

Arowan's four friends were torn between helping him and protecting Angel and Mouse. They split up. So with knives ready two of them swam to assist Arowan to try to rid him of the biting, evil serpents which were attacking him from every angle.

Arowan had to let go of Inanya's throat when he had hit the two serpents but he still had hold of her by the arm and he wasn't about to let go.

His two friends managed to slash a few of the slimy creatures but it seemed an impossible task as they were heavily outnumbered.

The two other friends had swum to Angel and Mouse and watched as the mass of serpents, Inanya and Arowan battled against eachother.

Mouse was motionless in Angel's arms, with blood still flowing like a watery ribbon from her head injury.

"Take her to the surface Angel, we need to help your dad." Shouted one of the friends.

Angel didn't need telling twice so she carefully cradled Mouse and they slowly drifted upwards and away from the murky, blood coloured water.

The ripped bodies of several serpents scattered the seabed but there were still enough of them to put up a terrible deadly fight.

Arowan was trying to keep hold of Inanya with one hand and slash at her with his knife with the other. Unfortunately he was failing at both; two serpents had clamped their sharp toothy mouths around the arm which held the knife and Inanya was pulling away from his other hand and whipping him savagely with her spiky tail.

Eventually she was free, having wrestled free from Arowan's hold on her. The five men were struggling to fend off the teeth and tails of the serpents and Inanya was watching, enjoying them losing.

What none of them saw through the murky, blood tainted water was an enormous shape slowly coming towards them all.

Arowan and his friends had sustained minor injuries so far but their energy was fading and they would need to surface soon, for air.

Inanya was satisfied that they would all be dead within minutes and swam to the seabed to retrieve The Trident. If it hadn't transformed her then it was unlikely that it would get the girl home but she wasn't taking any chances.

She picked it up and just looked at it. So many years of dreaming and hoping for this day and it had all been a total waste of time and disappointment. Lost in her thoughts, she didn't notice the huge set of teeth and an equally huge mouth that were just behind her!

The 20 foot monster picked up speed as it swam silently

and purposefully in her direction, the bloodied water tantalising it's taste buds.

Before Inanya even knew it was there, the shark shifted gear once more and sped through the last few feet of water with its jaw wide open, and CRUNCH!

There was a strangled scream.

The Trident dropped back down to the seabed.

The shark and the Serpent Queen were gone.

All that remained of the Serpent Queen was the tip of a spiny black tail laying several feet away from The Trident.

Suddenly aware that something important had happened Arowan, his friends and the serpents stopped mid-fight.

The serpents unclamped their jaws from whatever body parts they had hold of and almost spun into a frenzy again, looking for their Queen. They finally spotted what was left of her, and now in an almost trance like state, drifted down to the bottom of the sea.

Arowan and his four exhausted friends knew they had to take this opportunity to escape. They carefully swam for The Trident, the serpents not even noticing them.

Arowan scooped it up and together they swam to the surface where they all gulped in huge lung full's of air.

Arowan searched for Angel and Mouse but they were nowhere to be seen.

His heart froze. What if the creature who had savaged Inanya had got to Angel and Mouse first!

"Arowan, over there!" Shouted one of his trusted friends.

"Where, I can't see?" The swell of the water was blocking his view but as he pushed himself high out of the water he finally saw Angel on the back of Torpedo and Mouse slumped over Discus. They were slowly making their way to the shore.

"Good girl." Muttered Arowan.

The five weary men, conscious of their own cuts and bruises, swam as fast as they could to catch up and eventually all came together in the shallows.

The men lifted Mouse from the turtles back and Angel clambered off the dolphin. She gave them both an affectionate pat and they shot off together, back into deeper waters.

"She's still breathing dad but hasn't moved since she hit her head." Said Angel.

"We need to get her to Bichir, get her changed into her normal clothes and get her and The Trident back to the magic tree!" Sighed Arowan.

"She told us before that when she returned to her world the last time, that her cuts and scrapes disappeared when she got back to her world dad, but I'm worried that this is a lot worse and she may not recover?"

"It's crossed my mind too Angel. We just have to hope that the power of The Trident is strong enough to heal her as well as get her back home."

"Do you think it will work?"

"I'm hoping it will after what happened when she first touched it in the Cave of Thrones."

"But it didn't change Inanya dad?"

"No, it didn't but she was pure evil, and deserved what she got."

Arowan told Angel about what they had and hadn't seen and what was left of the Serpent Queen as they all carefully swam back up river, gently carried Mouse through the tunnel and onto the beach, in Bichir.

They were immediately surrounded by concerned villagers wanting to know what happened and desperately wanting to help in any way.

"Angel do you have her own clothes and shoes?" Asked Arowan.

"They're in my dwelling."

"Ok everyone, let's give her some space." The villagers drifted apart and the group moved slowly towards Angel's dwelling, where they lay her on the rocky bed.

"Go and get your girl friends to help you Angel, clean her wounds and get her changed." Arowan instructed.

The men retreated and followed Angel onto the beach. They told the expectant villagers what had happened while Angel sought out Vimba and Mora to help her. They scooped up some clean fresh water from the pool in a bowl and went back to Mouse.

The girls managed to cradle her head and wash away the blood from the deep cut on the back of her skull. Mora went back to the pool and got some more clean water to wash away the blood from Mouse's face and hair.

The three girls struggled to get Mouse out of her wet, snug fitting 'costume' made of seaweed but they soon had her changed back into her own clothes.

As Angel, Vimba and Mora emerged from the dwelling Arowan asked "Has she moved at all?"

"No dad."

"We need to get her to the magic tree as soon as possible."

Angel grabbed his arm as he went to pas her, "How is Tang?"

"He's doing well Angel. It's a long story but it turns out he was in cahoots with Inanya and once she had finished using him, she tried to have him killed!"

"What? Tang?"

"Yes, Tang. I think he has learnt his lesson the hardest way possible. He was lucky the serpents left him for dead in a watery ditch."

"I just can't believe it dad."

"All because he was jealous of Mouse. He wanted her to go back to her world so you and he could be best friends again."

"Really? All this happened because he was jealous!"

"It seems so but like I said, we've only heard the outline of what happened, and he's mortified at what he did."

"I'm so annoyed with him," growled Angel, " but I'm glad he's better."

"He's far from better just yet, but he'll be ok, in time."

"Let's hope Mouse is that lucky."

"Better get going. You'll have to lead the way, back to where you first saw her. The tree will be near there somewhere."

"Ok, let's get going then."

The villagers had been busy and had fashioned a small stretcher so that Mouse could be comfortably moved to the magic tree.

Arowan and his friends had been for a quick swim and washed their injuries, which thankfully were nothing more than a few bite marks and a few scratches.

All the villagers surrounded Mouse who looked like she was doing nothing more than sleeping on the stretcher. They all said their goodbyes, some out loud and some silently, to the astonishing young girl who had been part of their lives for a brief time. And all of them hoped she would be ok once she got back to her world.

They lifted up the stretcher and carried her above their heads as they made their way in the pool towards the waterfall. Some of the villagers had gathered large leaves and were now making a shield in the water so that Mouse could get through the waterfall and not get too wet.

It wasn't long before a motionless but fairly dry Mouse was being carried away from Bichir and into the jungle.

There were enough villagers with weapons to protect them if necessary but thankfully not a leaf or a branch moved out of place.

Angel lead the party through the jungle, the same way she had raced from Mouse, the very first day. That day seemed like weeks ago as they trudged through the dense jungle foliage. Angel always stayed close to the edge of the trees when she was in the jungle - close to the beach, close to water and only a quick sprint to safety if the occasion arose. She was not used to venturing further into the trees so it took some time to pinpoint the exact location of where Mouse could have emerged from.

After several wrong turns they finally found the magic tree - it stood out like a sore thumb! It's sparse, dry dangly leaves in total contrast to the thick, lush vegetation which surrounded it.

Angel held the leaves aside as the men brought Mouse inside the trees cocoon. They lay the stretcher onto the ground and Angel watched as they lovingly lifted Mouse off and onto the ground. They tried to position her as comfortably as possible.

Angel wandered around the tree to find some more leaves to put under Mouse's head and came across her artists box. "Dad, look!"

Angel had opened the pad and stared at the picture of Inanya, the Serpent Queen.

"She must have been shaken up when she saw *that*." Said Arowan.

"Especially as she'd drawn a beautiful mermaid in the first place."

"Poor little thing."

"I'll just rest the box and the pad next to her."

Angel put the box and pad down and then scooped up some leaves and put them gently under her head. She then pulled the bracelet from her pouch and put it around Mouse's wrist, and lay the string of shells at her side.

"I'll never forget you Mouse." She said.

One of the men bought The Trident into the inner circle of the tree and laid it down beside her.

Arowan bent down and kissed the top of her head, "It's been an enormous pleasure knowing you young lady."

They all said their goodbyes and left Mouse and The Trident inside the tree, while they stood outside and waited.

Within moments the tree began to come alive.

It sparkled.

It swayed.

It whooshed.

Arowan, Angel and their friends stood back in amazement as they watched the spectacular sight before them; the branches almost reached out to them as the swaying continued, the sparkly, glittery lights dazzling them.

Then as quickly as it had begun, it was over.

They'd all been holding their breath, hoping and praying for Mouse's safe return to her own world. They let out huge sighs and then almost instantly held their breath again as they moved towards the tree. All hoping that The Trident had just been 'choosy' about who it had worked for, and that it had the strength to make Mouse well again.

Angel was the first to approach the tree.

She silently held out her hand and moved the branches apart.

She gasped.

For there, under the tree, was The Trident and .....

THE END

Lightning Source UK Ltd.
Milton Keynes UK
UKOW03f0909160214

226534UK00011B/373/P